LOVE LIKE AIR

Hearts in Hendricks Book Three

D.E. MALONE

For information, contact dawnemalone@gmail.com
Love Like Air, First Edition
Copyright © 2019 D.E. Malone
All rights reserved.
ISBN (paperback) 978-0-9903242-9-4
(ebook) 978-0-9903242-8-7
Cover designed by Seedlings Design Studio

Summary: Donut shop owner Debi Thomas fights to keep a mining operation from encroaching on her family's homestead and wonders if Mick Graham, the man who has suddenly captured her heart, is also helping the mine's owner acquire the property.

Listen to its simple strain,
Peaceful as the falling rain,
A breath that gives the branches sway
To pass along a languid day.

— Silas Penn

Chapter One

❧

Even with the pastry cases fully stocked and Lake Superior shining like a liquid jewel through her shop's front window, Debi Thomas's day had started off all wrong.

She'd already glanced at the ceramic donut clock on the wall three times in the last ten minutes, and it wasn't even eight o'clock. All she longed for was to sink into her couch with a mug of tea and a foot warmer in the form of her bull terrier, Harley. Instead, she was forced to listen to the five guys at the window table discuss the mining potential of her property—her *home*—like she wasn't standing fifteen feet away. Debi needed to leave before her mood went nuclear and Debi's Donuts turned into ground zero.

Behind her, the timer on the counter rang incessantly. Debi was too busy to turn it off, too busy eavesdropping on their conversation. She held her hand up as if the gesture would silence the buzzer, but then she realized she was shushing an inanimate object, and grabbed it off the back counter to flip the *off* button.

When Debi turned around, one of the men, stocky and bearded, stood at the counter. He had an air about him like the others, aloof and slightly amused.

"How are *you* today?" he asked while looking in the donut case. The light inside the case highlighted his sunburnt nose and cheeks.

"Wonderful. How about yourself?" Debi gave him what felt like her best smile. She uncrossed her arms, smoothed the front of her apron, and folded her hands together on the counter. Trying to be pleasant while silently fuming took some effort.

"You've got a regular Robert Frost somewhere in town," he said, still focused on the inside of the case. The tray of jelly-filled donuts had his full attention. He was a semi-regular, one of the new geologists at Lost Pine Mine. His name was Don, maybe? Or was it Lon?

"Excuse me?"

He straightened and held out a half sheet of notebook paper. The coffee stain in one corner made the paper brittle, and it crunched when she took it. The handwriting, slanted and tall, reminded Debi of her mother's grocery lists when Debi was young. Distracted, she read it quickly. The poem was about donuts. She couldn't recall any Robert Frost poems about donuts. At least not the poems she'd read.

"Found it under the napkin dispenser. Friend of yours?"

Again, his question caught her off guard. Debi met his eyes and realized he toyed with her. The creases around his eyes deepened.

"No. I have no idea who wrote this."

"Shame. Whoever it is has some talent."

"And you know poetry?" Her tone came out clipped before she caught herself. *Calm down.*

"Not at all. It just has a nice sound to it."

Debi stuffed the poem into her apron's pocket. "What can I get you?"

His chest rose and fell with a deep breath, probably realizing she wasn't in the mood for his chitchat. "Two chocolate glazed to go."

She busied herself with getting his order together as fast as possible. Despite the crowded bakery, which normally perked her up, the current clientele left her rankled. Executives from the mine were never a joyous bunch. Debi caught her reflection in the mirror hanging over the back counter. The dark slashes of her eyebrows pinched together. *Goodness. I'll scare everyone away if I don't start smiling.*

Holly Prater, her part-timer, sidled up next to Debi as she plucked donuts from the case. Holly's blond ponytail swished against Debi's shoulder as the girl leaned toward her.

"I have dough in the mixer ready to go. You could take over if you want a change of scenery," Holly whispered.

Debi kept her back turned to the man and spoke in a hushed tone. "That's probably best. I feel a rant coming on. Yelling at customers wouldn't be good for business, would it?"

Holly giggled. "That'd be the talk of the town. I can see the headline now:

'Bakery Owner Assaults Clientele with Donuts.'"

Debi cringed. In a low voice, she said, "Yeah. Sadly, it's not so impossible to imagine. I'll finish up here then head back."

A high school senior, Holly had worked at the donut shop since the day she was old enough to have a worker's permit. She'd come into the bakery most mornings since Christmas break as part of an intern program at the high school for kids interested in small business opportunities. She was sharp, a go-getter. Debi would miss her when she left for college in August.

At the register, Debi handed the man his donuts.

"Thank you," he said, opening the bag to smell the contents. The corners of his mouth lifted. When he handed over a five-dollar bill, he hummed the theme song to "Rocky."

In spite of herself, Debi laughed. Her donuts elicited the funniest reactions sometimes.

"I'm Lon, by the way. We haven't formally met."

"Nice to meet you, Lon." Debi softened a bit and handed back his change.

"I feel like I have to apologize for them." He hooked his thumb over his shoulder. "If it's any consolation, this place is better than the board room for hashing things out."

"Oh?" She glanced at the table again. One of the men talked so loudly a few of the other customers looked their way and frowned. *They're probably hashing out how they're going to bully me into giving up my property.* She looked back at Lon. "I'm happy to hear you're comfortable here."

"We're probably scaring away customers." Lon made it sound more like a question than a statement.

Debi breathed deeply to quell her immediate reply. "Don't worry about it. You're livening the place up is all." She couldn't help but notice the way his gaze lingered on her a little longer than normal.

He closed the bag and gave her a slight nod.

"I'll try to hurry them up."

Lon rejoined the group at the table, giving her one last glance over his shoulder. Debi blew the air out of her cheeks as their voices rose again with Lon back in the mix. Their lighthearted banter as they stuffed her donuts into their yapping mouths like hyenas grated on her. Yes, Holly was right. Debi needed to work in the kitchen until the group left.

"You did well," Holly whispered as she unfolded a donut box and slid open the case. "Did he say anything? You know, about your land?"

"Oh, he wouldn't dare. They never would to my face. Sooner or later, I'll get a letter from someone at the mine. A request for a meeting. It's happened before; it'll happen again." Debi wiped her hands on her apron. "But that's why they come in here to talk. So I can hear them. They do it to intimidate me, I think."

"They can't do that, can they? Take away your property?"

"Nope, not without me selling it to them. But that won't stop them from trying to make me leave."

"Maybe you should get an attorney," Holly said, plucking cake donuts out of the case to fill the box.

"I will. If it comes to the point where they're doing more than flapping their mouths in here. For now, it's only annoying. I want to refuse them service, but that's not good for business either."

Holly closed the lid on the box. "There's nothing worse than smiling when you don't want to."

"It's easier with practice." Debi demonstrated, smiling with all her teeth as she headed back into the kitchen.

Holly laughed. "That was scary."

Debi was in the back room not two minutes before the doorbell chimed. She poked her head around the corner. It was Darcy Conti, manager of Blueberry Point Lodge. She couldn't ignore Darcy. She was one of Debi's favorite people. The shop had provided donuts for Sturgeon Widows Tours for years, and now that the tour company owned the Lodge, Debi gained another venue for her baked goods. Darcy called in the next week's order every Wednesday. And if there was anyone who could brighten up the place, it was Darcy.

"Hey, lady," Darcy said, squinting to see the coffee flavors of the day on the board. Debi had already poured her a cup and slid it across the counter.

"No charge."

"Thank you." Darcy glanced behind her, probably looking for familiar faces. Everyone knew Darcy. And of course the mine guys noticed her. She waved at them. The ones whose eyes she caught waved back in unison. Funny, Debi mused. She worked a crowd like a maestro conducts an orchestra.

Darcy leaned forward conspiratorially and said under her breath, "Your current clientele is a good-looking group."

"I wish they were as nice to interact with as they were to look at."

"Yeah, I hear they can be a surly bunch," she said in the same lighthearted way she'd pass on a compliment or narrate one of her tours. Her dark eyes grew large. "Anyway, I have news!" She held out her hand to show off a marquis-cut diamond ring on her finger.

"Wait a minute. That looks like an engagement ring." Debi rested her elbows on the counter, taking Darcy's hand to get a closer look.

"It is! Isn't it something?"

"It's about time Sean asked you. Congratulations!"

Darcy snorted. "If it was up to him, I'd still be waiting. I asked *him*!"

"That's even better." Debi straightened again. "Have you set a date?"

"Sort of. We nailed down the season at least. Sometime in late summer."

"The weather should be ideal."

Darcy pressed her palms together. "And you'll do the cake, right?"

"I'd never bake again if you didn't choose me."

"Wonderful! I told Sean you had one more wedding cake in you even if you don't do them anymore."

"Anything for you guys."

Darcy leaned forward again. She tucked a mass of black curls behind one ear. "That's not the real reason I'm here," she whispered.

"What is it?"

"We're going to start something a little different at the Lodge—themed weekend events for singles."

Debi lifted her eyebrows.

"I know, I know. I can just hear the group at the coffeehouse talking about what kind of business I'm running." Darcy added quickly, "But it's going to be so much fun!"

"Ha! Says the outsider from the big city. The locals aren't exactly progressive folks." Debi didn't worry about Darcy taking offense. They had an easy friendship with a shared talent for speaking their minds.

Darcy dismissed the comment with an impatient wave. "I'm excited about this! I don't care what they think."

"I can't imagine being matched with anyone for five minutes let alone a whole weekend. Count me out."

"I was going to ask if you'd be willing to give it a trial run. You know, to test the concept?"

"Honey, I'm better at making sweets than being someone's sweetheart."

"Total nonsense. You're funny, smart, and you make people feel special. Besides, you're not committed to hanging out with one person exclusively. It's more of an extended date with a bunch of like-minded people."

"That's even more frightening. I'm too much of a pain, especially when a man gets underfoot. I don't have the temperament for that anymore."

"What? You're only a little older than me."

"I'm still recovering."

Darcy gave her a knowing look. "I understand." Resigned, she let out a sigh. "I'll take you off the list then."

"Thank you. Besides, you have the only decent single man left in the whole county."

"I know! That's why I have to get this marriage thing

finalized." Darcy laughed. She took a pocket calendar from her bag and opened it on the counter. "But I do need some custom treats to match the themes. The second weekend in June will bring together a bunch of bikers."

"As in motorcycles?"

She chuckled again. "No, cyclists."

Debi tapped her chin with her finger, thinking. "How about my granola breakfast muffins and jersey-shaped sugar cookies? I could also do mini carrot cupcakes with a spoked wheel decoration on top."

"Yes, that would be perfect. I'll let you know when I get final numbers."

When Darcy left the shop, Debi turned her attention back to the Lost Pine Mine guys taking over her bakery. They seemed in no hurry to leave. Outside, the sky had clouded over as if sensing Debi's turbulent mood. The batter waited for her in the mixer still, so with one last glance at the mine workers, she left Holly in charge of the counter. Debi needed a distraction before her lightened mood, courtesy of Darcy, turned black again.

Chapter Two

❧

Mick Graham was grateful a whole month had passed since his last visit to the principal's office at Broman County Junior High School. Still, his daughter's cavalier attitude about her latest offense did little to quell his frustration. When would the behavior issues stop?

A steady wind pushed against his back while they walked to his truck parked in one of the visitor spots. He fought the wind as he pulled open the truck's door, and it almost caught his foot when it slammed the door shut behind him. Stella struggled to get into the truck, too, fighting the violent wind, but finally climbed into the passenger seat beside him. Outside was a stark contrast to the chilly silence inside the truck. Mick took a few extra moments to gaze through the windshield at the white-necked birch trees swaying in the wind in front of them.

So resilient.

He closed his eyes, imagining he was one of those trees, steeling himself against the onslaught of Stella's anger.

I have to be resilient too. For Stella.

"It wasn't like I was going to leave school. I mean, I *wanted* to, but I'm not stupid."

Stella sighed and leaned against the car door, pressing her forehead against the glass. The condensation from her breath clouded the window with each silent exhale. "I didn't feel like sitting in class anymore."

"You walking out of class wasn't the only thing that happened this afternoon as I understand it." Mick glanced at Stella as he pulled out on Highway 61.

It took her awhile to answer. Finally, she said in a small voice, "No, it wasn't."

"Well, either Mrs. Reil didn't want to repeat what you said or she didn't know. What did you say to her?"

"Only that I can learn more in five minutes from my grandmother than I can in an hour and twenty minutes in her class. And she didn't hear me because I said it under my breath."

"Mrs. Reil said you were acting in a threatening way too."

Stella kept her eyes on some distant point outside the car, but her jaw dropped and she shook her head in disbelief.

"So what did you do that made her feel threatened?"

She looked at him. "I just got in her face is all. Too close, I guess. Like this." She leaned over and touched noses with him.

He almost smiled at being eye to eye with her, but then Stella would note his weakness and he'd lose his edge.

"Getting in your teacher's personal space is not cool." Mick leaned back against the headrest and blew air out of his cheeks. "You go for the jugular, don't you?"

Stella was silent.

"What are we going to do about this?"

He looked over at her again when she didn't answer. Stella's dark hair was pulled back into a ponytail, exposing her profile. Already he could see the emerging young woman, even at twelve years old. The lines of her face were becoming more angular as her soft childlike features melted away. She was a good mixture of her mother and him. She had his coloring, dark hair and fair skin, but her mother's striking eye color that reminded him of birch leaves in October, that in-between color as they turned from green to gold.

"I can't wait to see what the school's punishment will be for this little incident. Two-day suspension? A written apology to everyone in class and their parents for the disruption?" He turned off the highway and headed up High Road toward home.

"No way!"

"Who knows?" he said, glancing at her. If a written apology drew that kind of reaction from her, maybe Mick would suggest it to Mrs. Reil if it wasn't already on the table. Stella deserved it.

Stella huffed and went back to staring out the window. "Everyone is so sensitive."

"No, they're not. You belong in school, in *class*. And you

show respect to people. That's not negotiable. And what's this about your grandmother signing you out last week?"

Stella lifted a shoulder. "She does it all the time."

"All the time?!"

"Not *all* the time. Maybe once every couple weeks."

Mick knew Gretchen Hinsdorff took her granddaughter to lunch on occasion but didn't realize it had become a ritual.

"It's not a big deal. We go to lunch. Then she takes me to work."

"What for?"

"So I can watch what she does. So I can take over for her some day."

"This is unreal," he said under his breath. Gretchen had been trying to undermine him since the day he met her. Mick figured it would have ended after Raila's death, but it only seemed to have gotten worse. Stella was the pawn, whether or not his daughter realized it. Mick didn't doubt Gretchen loved doting on her only granddaughter, but he suspected Gretchen enjoyed rubbing her close relationship with Stella in his face even more.

They rode in silence for a while before Stella spoke in a low voice.

"It doesn't hurt anything, Dad. They don't teach this real-world stuff in English, you know."

"You're right. They don't. But your grandmother also isn't giving you a well-rounded education either. She's not teaching you how to write a paper. She's not teaching you a foreign language or geometry or how to read a map."

"Actually she *is* showing me how to read maps. There's a

new mining prospect she's interested in buying. She has maps all over her office."

Mick clamped his jaw shut and gripped the steering wheel tighter. Any discussion turned into a debate. He was finished for now.

Up ahead, a flash of yellow caught Mick's attention. As he got closer, the yellow became a woman in a hooded raincoat. Black rubber boots. Chestnut hair spilled from underneath the hood. She was getting her mail, her dog by her side. He slowed as they passed her so he wouldn't accidentally splash her on the rain-soaked road. She raised her hand. Mick waved back.

Debi Thomas.

He craned his neck to glance at Debi in the rearview mirror until he noticed Stella staring at him.

"What?"

"Why don't you ask her out, Dad? Don't pretend you don't want to."

"Wait...what? Ask Debi Thomas out?" *Where was this coming from?*

Stella threw her hands up and looked out the window. Her breath fogged the window again as she spoke. "There you go again."

"What's that supposed to mean?"

"Clueless."

"Excuse me? I think that's kind of uncalled for. Especially in light of your current situation."

"Please."

His patience was almost gone. "What has gotten into you lately?"

Stella continued looking out the window and shook her head. Lately she was wound like a spring. One wrong word, a look, and most of the time, trivial inconveniences, like a missing button or a dropped spoon set her off. Mick found himself holding his breath around her; the tension was sometimes that palpable.

And what's more, he'd never mentioned Debi Thomas, let alone designs about dating her. Adding another person to his life when he couldn't even manage his own daughter was all he needed. Besides, Debi never gave him a second look in all the years he and Stella had been steady customers at her shop. It wasn't like he missed the sign either. Clearly, she wasn't interested.

"Listen. I'm going to throw a pizza together for dinner, then we're gonna talk. A serious talk. None of this chip-on-your-shoulder, silent-treatment stuff anymore."

Stella glanced at him with raised eyebrows. "Or what?"

He met her challenge with a look of his own. "Don't, Stella."

She must have decided the tone in his voice meant business because she sank back against the seat and stared straight ahead. The grim set of her lips meant she'd given up the fight for now.

"Dad! Watch out!"

Mick gripped the wheel tightly and instinctively jerked it to the right, onto the shoulder, even before he noticed the vehicle ahead veering too close to them. His other arm shot out to keep Stella from pitching forward, even though her belt kept her right where she belonged. They bumped along the uneven shoulder, through potholes, pitched in their seats until Mick slowed down to a stop. He didn't see the truck as much as he heard it, the water hissing under its tires, barreling past him so quickly his truck shuddered. It had been a blur beside them, and then the red taillights were in his rearview mirror, disappearing around the curve and out of sight.

"He wasn't even on his side of the road! Jerk!"

His heart still jackhammering in his chest, Mick laid his forehead against the steering wheel. At least Stella directed the flashpoint of her anger at someone besides him for once.

"Did you see him? He almost hit us!"

"Yeah, I saw him. Wish I could have gotten his plate number though. I didn't even notice what color it was, did you?"

Stella whirled around in her seat, looking out the back window, as if she'd get Mick the information by sheer will. The truck was long gone though, probably halfway to town by now.

"No, I didn't."

Mick glanced again in his rearview mirror. The wet spray stirred up was settling down, but Debi Thomas's yellow coat caught his attention. Even from a distance Mick could tell by her movements something wasn't right.

He put the truck in reverse, easing it backward along the shoulder, and stopped at the edge of her driveway near the mailbox. He rolled down his window.

"Are you okay?"

It was a silly thing to ask because as soon as he spoke, it was clear things were decidedly *not* okay. The raincoat, before a sunny beacon on such a dull day, was now mottled with mud, along with her hair, which hung in dripping gray tendrils. Debi's face was contorted with rage.

"I can't...even speak....I-I'm that *mad*," she said, her voice shaking. She swiped at her coat in vain, but it only spread the mud to parts yet untouched. "Speed limit signs mean nothing to them *ever*! If anything, they speed up when they fly past my house."

"They" were the Lost Pine Mine people, the only ones who'd be coming down that stretch of road, down the northeast fork of Lost Pine Road from the mine. The fork met a hundred yards up from her driveway, becoming a single road that ran five miles down to Hendricks. His house sat at the end of the northwest fork, up the road another mile, in the midst of Sheevy's Lake State Park.

She lifted her arm slowly, wincing as she raised it to chest level. "I think I've wrenched my shoulder. That truck blew me back against the mailbox." Debi looked around. "Oh no! Where's Harley? He must have gotten spooked."

"He ran up our fork," Stella offered, pointing ahead.

Mick came around to the other side of the truck to open the back door of the quad cab. "Hop in."

"What?" Debi took a step back. "I'll get your truck dirty."

Mick looked up the road. "That's the least of our worries. Let's go catch Harley."

Stella scrambled over the console to climb into the backseat.

"Here, you get in the front seat," Stella said to Debi.

Debi winced when she tried grabbing the handle to help herself into the truck.

"I can't do it with this shoulder." She gritted her teeth while she clutched the arm.

He didn't like seeing her in pain. "Can I help?"

Debi's eyes widened, probably wondering what he had in mind. "Sure."

He scooped her up, setting her gently into the front seat. Stella sat silently, her wide eyes darting between Debi and him. His daughter's dating reference made moments ago hung in the air for a few seconds as he and Stella exchanged glances, but then Debi settled into her seat without another word, and Mick closed the door.

Chapter Three

Harley was halfway to Mick's house up the
northwest fork before they caught up to him in
the truck. Debi rolled her window down and
called the dog, but when he saw the unfamiliar truck
coming toward him, he only sped up. Finally, Mick stopped.
Debi opened the truck door and called him again. This time
the dog paused long enough for Debi to slide out of her seat
so the black-and-white dog recognized her. His ears pasted
against his head, Harley wagged timidly as she approached
him. Mick helped boost Harley into the front seat with her.
The dog barely fit in the space at her feet, but he didn't
seem to mind with Stella cooing at him from the backseat.

Stella reached over to tickle the dog under his chin.
"He's so cute."

Debi kept a steady hand on the dog's collar so he
wouldn't launch himself into the backseat with Stella. He

was a sucker for baby talk. "That's his only saving grace at the moment," Debi said.

They rode in silence for several minutes until Mick turned into the half-circle drive in front of his cedar-sided ranch. He met Debi on the other side as she opened her door. Debi readily took his arm as she slid out of the truck, pain shooting up her arm like an electrical current.

She held her breath, clamping her lips together as Mick helped across the driveway toward the house. "You don't have to worry—"

"Nonsense. You're hurt and upset. I—we can't drop you off at your house looking like this, feeling the way you do."

He led her inside, holding her one good arm, and while she stood in his entryway, dripping and cursing under her breath, he rounded up some towels. When he offered them to her and watched while Debi squeezed the dampness from her hair, crossing his arms and shifting from one foot to the other, he looked too awkward for a man standing in his own house.

"I'll get some dry clothes," he said and disappeared down the hall before she could protest.

The room in front of her was large and rustic. Its light wood-paneled walls gave it a sunny air, and braided rugs covering the stone-tiled floor added a zing of color. A large bank of windows looked out toward the woods on the opposite wall. Closer to her, family photos decorated the wall above an iron credenza. She stepped closer. Mick with Stella. Stella with two girls of similar age. Mick in a military uniform. A wedding photo.

Mick was back, startling her. He handed her a pile of clothes. "Here's some dry things."

Debi took them from him, giving him a long look, until Mick realized she didn't know where the bathroom was.

"Sorry," he said, pointing down the hall. "That way."

Behind her, Stella came inside, dumped her book bag on the floor, and flopped onto the couch across the room. Debi didn't miss the frown turning the corners of Mick's mouth downward as his daughter passed by him. Now was a good time to leave the room.

In the bathroom, she rinsed the mud and grit from her hair, towel-drying it as best she could while stewing about almost getting run over. The first thing she'd do when she got back home would be to give the mine office a call and report one of their employees almost killed her.

Once out of her soiled coat and pants and wearing the dry clothes, Debi's mood improved. She fingered the waves in her hair once more in front of the mirror before she switched off the light.

Mick's and Stella's voices carried down the hall.

"Well, that was convenient."

"What are you talking about?"

"The whole Mick-to-the-Rescue event."

"Don't start again. Especially with her here. And I'm Dad, not Mick."

"Whatever."

Debi paused mid-step inside the room. They were talking about *her*. Heat overcame her face. It was too late to retrace her steps since Mick and Stella noticed her in unison.

Debi shrank back. "I, uh—sorry. I didn't mean to surprise you."

Stella's expression was a mixture of annoyance and horror when she saw Debi. Something had triggered Stella, and the ferocity of her look shocked Debi.

Stella turned to her father, gaping at him. "Seriously, Dad?"

Mick looked equally horrified, but it was directed at Stella's outburst. "I think it's time for you to calm down in another part of the house," he said in a low tone.

Stella was already rising from the couch. "My pleasure!"

The girl stormed off in a flurry of mumbled words and curtains of black hair.

When a door slammed somewhere in the house, Debi came farther into the room.

"Did I do something?"

His expression was apologetic. "No, I did."

She waited for him to explain.

Finally, he said, "That shirt." He gestured to the one she wore, the one he'd given her to change into. "It was Raila's. My...wife."

Debi looked down at the tee shirt with "Property of University of Michigan Athletics" across the front. Now she understood.

He went on. "I wasn't thinking. And anyway, she's extra sensitive. Typical reaction to anything these days—last serving of cereal, a hangnail, the wind blowing—"

"I get it. Thanks for the change of clothes." She moved closer to the warm stove, holding her hands out. Even that slight move made her grimace. "I'll make sure they come back."

He noticed her reaction. "Sit here," he said.

Mick pulled the armchair closer to the stove. He'd found a heating pad for her shoulder and a bottle of ibuprofen. He settled on the brick hearth where he stoked the coals when they died down. Debi curled into the chair, pulled her feet under her, and carefully arranged the pad onto her shoulder. Then she wrapped the quilt around her and sighed.

Mick Graham and Stella had been coming into her shop for years. But aside from the typical banter she shared with most of her regulars, she'd never interacted with Mick Graham outside the store. They simply never crossed paths. With the drama of the speeding truck behind her and the fire's warmth coaxing her to relax, Debi turned her attention to the man in front of her. He was handsome enough. A shock of black hair fell askew in no particular style but framed his angular face in a roguish sort of way. He was neither tall or of a slight frame, owning an average-sized build for someone who worked outside for a living clearing trails, building fences, and plowing snow, depending on the season. A wave of self-consciousness hit her when she realized she'd been staring at him, and he'd noticed. She smiled and looked back at the fire.

"How long have you worked for the park?" she asked hurriedly. It was a stupid question, random, given the circumstances, but she needed to say something, anything to keep him from staring. Besides, she already knew the answer.

Mick glanced down at his shoes, thinking. "Oh, I imagine it's been thirteen years now. First job out of college."

"You must like it enough to stick around." The awkwardness of this conversation knew no bounds. "In Hendricks, I mean."

"Not many places for a geology major to work around these parts. Besides, Stella's in school." He shrugged. "How's it feel?"

Clearly, he didn't want to talk about himself. She moved her arm and tried lifting it to shoulder height, but she could barely move it away from her side.

"It's tightening up, I'm afraid."

Mick shook his head. "I'd give whomever it was a citation if it were within my jurisdiction."

"Wouldn't do any good. Gretchen would just pay the ticket, and they'd continue speeding." As the owner of Mesabi Holdings and the Lost Pine Mine prospect, Gretchen Hinsdorff was above it all: playing fair, compromising, obeying speed limits. "She's ruthless."

"True."

Debi glanced at him, immediately regretting her words when she heard the bitterness in his voice. She'd forgotten who Gretchen was to Mick. After Gretchen's daughter and Mick's wife, Raila, had passed away years ago, the contention between mother-in-law and son-in-law grew. The veil of civility they maintained before Raila's sickness fell away once Raila was no longer around to act as the buffer. At least that's what she picked up through the grapevine.

Aside from the occasional small talk over the donut case, Debi didn't know much about Raila other than she was a bit reserved and had a fondness for coconut cream pie. On the contrary, Mick and little Stella had come in weekly, which changed to twice weekly in more recent years.

Harley got up from his spot in the corner and sat in front of her, balancing on his haunches to put his paws up on her lap. She scratched him between the ears, and he closed his eyes for a few contented moments, seemingly anxious to leave the stranger's house.

"At least I have one good arm to pet you with," she mused aloud. No sooner had she dropped her hand than Harley nudged it, wanting more of her attention.

"Maybe you should see the doctor if it's not better by tomorrow," Mick said, his brows drawing together when she tucked her arm slowly at her side again.

"I don't even want to think about doctors and therapy and arm slings. The season is just getting started."

Hendricks was very much a seven-month-on, five-month-off community. During winter, most of the art studios and a few of the smaller cafes closed with the drop off in clientele. She had debated about doing the same the last few years, but there were plenty of locals left from November through April to make staying open worthwhile. Though the high season was great for the bank account, she loved the change in her customer base during cold months more. The familiar faces visiting on a regular basis gave her a chance to renew the relationships she missed out on when the donut shop thrummed with summer tourists.

She caught Mick staring again. Debi smiled. "I owe you a year's supply of free donuts for this."

Her joke seemed to put him at ease, because he chuckled and patted his stomach. "I won't take you up on that, though it's tempting." His gaze rested on her momentarily before he looked away again. Mick seemed unsure, almost shy. It was sort of charming. Debi caught herself grinning before she ducked her head.

"How do you look so good owning a place like that?" he asked, but the boldness of the words registered on Mick's face almost instantly. "I'm sorry. That was rude." He rubbed his hands on the sides of his jeans and turned his attention to the fire again.

Debi laughed. "Don't worry about it. I sometimes wonder myself. And just so you know, I hear a version of the same comment every single day. I've grown immune to it."

He wouldn't look at her now. Was his face red, or was it the glow from the fire?

"Anyway, I should probably get back." She looked toward her bag of clothes sitting in the tiled entryway.

Mick rubbed the side of his face, the stubble of his whiskers making a soft scratching sound as he studied her.

"Are you sure? It will only get worse before it gets better. I could take you into town for an x-ray."

Debi waved him off. "I'm willing it to not give me any trouble. Stubbornness and a bottle of ibuprofen will be my best friends for a while."

So they left the cabin with Harley willingly tagging along, and Mick helped them back into his truck for the five-minute drive back to her place. He hummed as he drove.

Debi couldn't place the tune, though it was a familiar one, and she wracked her brain all night to name the melody, humming it herself off and on until she was ready to turn off the light on her nightstand.

It would come to her eventually.

Chapter Four

Aline snaked to the door of the donut shop when Mick walked in behind Stella on Tuesday morning. If it weren't for the scent of fried yeast and coffee, Mick would have backed out the door and headed to the gas station for an apple fritter and a Styrofoam cup to go. But a stop at Debi's Donuts was his ritual. The shop had been his go-to place ever since he moved to Hendricks. This morning, it was apparently everyone else's favorite spot too.

Stella groaned and slumped. "This will take forever."

He put his hand on her shoulder. "Look on the bright side: Every minute we stand here is a minute you don't have to be at school."

"Good point," she said, tapping her index finger on her chin, thinking. "It's okay if I'm late."

"I'm joking. You're not going to be late."

Ahead of Stella, Matt Stetman waited in line. Matt was a

shorter, lighter version of his brother, Sean, and as talkative as his brother was quiet. Mick figured Matt was in his late twenties and in no hurry to settle down, judging by the number of women he'd seen him with on occasion at Red's Tavern. Still, Matt was the happy-go-lucky type who had something positive to say about everyone. It was easy to like a guy like Matt.

"How's my favorite park ranger today?" Matt asked around the toothpick bobbing between his teeth.

Mick noted the length of the line again. "Desperate for a donut like everyone else in town appears to be."

"Hey, I'm in survival mode here too. I need this like I need air to breathe." He looked to Stella. "How many hearts have you broken lately?"

Stella smiled from one side of her mouth. "All of them," she said under her breath.

"That's what I like to hear." He took the toothpick from his mouth when he looked back at Mick. "I'll be up one of these weekends when we get good weather to work on that fence."

Mick was still marveling that Matt drew a smile out of Stella. His daughter was obviously smitten. "Sounds good. I'll have the materials ready." Mick peered around Matt, at the gap in the line as the person ahead of him moved up to the counter. "Looks like your sweet tooth will be satisfied sooner rather than later."

Matt jumped ahead and became distracted by the donut case, a twelve-foot, wraparound display of all things sweet at Debi's Donuts. Mick had sampled everything in there, from the sprinkled chocolate eclairs to the bear claws and even the old-fashioned donuts, pumpkin or apple cider, it made no difference. Everything was mouthwatering.

He looked around the shop while he and Stella waited. It was easy to see why Debi's Donuts was a popular spot. In a word, the place was fun. For one, the donut theme spilled out of the cases and onto the walls with donut art done by North Shore artists. When Debi took over the business from her parents, she'd hired a few artist friends to paint dinner plate-sized donuts on one wall, setting the tone for the rest of the space. Mick remembered reading about the transformation in the newspaper. She'd replaced the nondescript tables with yellow-topped linoleum ones, along with matching chairs too. The clear vases of seasonal flowers, a wall of coffee mugs, and vintage pendant lights made the shop downright charming. Debi Thomas had a clear eye for design.

A few minutes later, he and Stella found a spot at a small table near the window. Stella wasn't due at school until after eight o'clock, and his appointment with the principal wasn't until eight thirty. He'd need his breakfast to settle before he met that challenge, thanks to Stella. Mick settled into a chair, watching the people waiting to place their orders. It was funny what a little sugar and a busy donut shop did to a person's mindset. Or maybe it was the donut shop owner who suddenly appeared at the counter, coming from the back kitchen.

He'd known Debi for more than thirteen years, yet it seemed like he'd met her for the first time last Thursday. That wasn't an earth-shattering realization on his part since ordering donuts at the counter twice a week didn't exactly count for deeply personal conversations. But there she was, behind the same pastry case, saying the exact same two words she said to everyone when they came to the counter —"Hey there!"—and it was like Debi Thomas was a newer, more thrilling version of herself. Her hair was a richer shade of chestnut, her eyes a cobalt blue like the cold water of Sheevy's Lake before it froze over for the winter. Even her laugh—*that laugh*—had taken on a musical quality that normally made everyone laugh themselves at its heartiness.

"Dad?"

"Huh?" He liked how Debi's eyes crinkled at the edges even when she wasn't smiling. Bright, enchanting. Even from across the room.

"What are you doing?"

Debi spotted him. She nodded a greeting.

"What?" His attention was back on Stella. Her eyebrows pinched together.

"You're holding your donut in midair and your mouth's open."

The eclair was indeed poised in front of his face.

Stella gave him a deadpan look. "That's embarrassing."

He sank his teeth into it with exaggerated gusto. "Never mind me," he said around the mouthful. "I was admiring its perfection before I indulged."

"You were not. Just because I'm twelve doesn't mean I'm stupid." Stella set her notebook on the table and looked pointedly over her shoulder at the front counter.

Mick set the donut down. "I've never for one second thought you were stupid. What's that you're studying?"

"Social studies. I have a quiz first hour."

"Are you ready?"

"Sort of. Can I quiz you?"

Mick squinted at her. "Aren't I the one who should be quizzing you?"

"It will help me learn." When he didn't respond, she sat up straight. "Okay, name three economic trends in Asia from 1000 to 1500."

When Mick looked at her blankly, Stella sighed. "C'mon, Dad. Long-distance trade, specialized jobs, scientific progress."

He threw his hands up. "Well, of course!"

His daughter smiled again. Two smiles within the hour. Call the Guinness Book of World Records.

When a steaming carafe appeared over his shoulder, and a black stream of coffee filled his almost empty mug, Mick's heartbeat quickened.

"You looked like you were on empty."

Debi.

She'd come up behind him after circling to the other tables. She walked around the table to face him. Her hair was swept back in a ponytail, curls fanning over one shoulder.

Mick cleared his throat. "You could tell all the way across the room? You're good." He sat back in his chair to get a better look at her.

"Honey, I can tell by looking at a person whether they're the cream-and-sugar type or take their coffee black. As far as knowing who needs a refill? That's beginner stuff."

Mick felt himself nodding like a bobblehead. He couldn't

take his eyes off her. Then he caught Stella staring. She rolled her eyes.

If Debi saw Stella's expression, she didn't let on. "I'd better continue my rounds. This is a rough crowd when they're not properly caffeinated."

"How's the arm?"

Debi smiled and lifted the carafe. "It still pours." She winked at him before she moved on to the next table.

He watched her over the top of his mug, a heated cloud washing over his face as he sipped. When his gaze shifted back to his daughter, Stella's eyes narrowed. That kid didn't miss much.

"See, you *do* want to date her."

"What, I can't talk to people now without you thinking I want to date them?" he said in a hushed tone. "Keep your voice down."

"Not everyone. Only her."

Mick polished off the donut, crumpled his napkin, and stood. "C'mon. It's getting late."

Stella closed her notebook. "You're in denial. And you want to get me out of here before I say something in front of her," she said, her chin tilted. She liked teasing him, especially when she thought she had him figured out. "You're scared, aren't you?"

"I have no idea where you get these ideas, but save them for writing class."

Stella slung her backpack over her shoulder as they left the shop. Only when they were safely outside, without an audience for Stella's verbal theatrics, did Mick breathe easy.

. . .

MICK SAT IN A CHAIR OUTSIDE PAUL PRICES'S office, waiting for Stella's principal to call him in. He didn't expect much to happen, truthfully. For as strict as Stella's teacher was—and rightly so, given his daughter's attitude lately—Price didn't have his staff's backs. Stella's last offense in March, another snide comment followed by crumpling a graded assignment and shooting it into the wastebasket from two rows over, earned her an office visit. The three times before that: office visits. Last week's incident was the first time he'd had to make an appointment to see Paul. Stella said Principal Price acted more like everyone's favorite uncle than a disciplinarian.

"Mick?"

Paul stood in the doorway and showed him into the office. Mick was surprised to see Stella's language arts teacher, Angie Reil, and Ben Melker, the school social worker, in the room as well. The two of them greeted Mick.

Uh-oh.

Paul settled in his chair. "I thought we could start by asking if you have any questions about Stella's latest incident."

Mick realized he was gripping the arms of his chair before he dropped them to his lap. His hands were sweating.

He glanced at Angie. "From what Stella told me, she talked back to you. And she also mentioned she was 'in your face' as she put it."

Angie nodded. "Correct. She was definitely challenging me."

"I'm sorry. We talked about it over the weekend. She regrets it."

Again, Angie acknowledged it but didn't say a word.

"Since this seems to be happening on a regular basis, I think it needs to be addressed in a different way," Paul said.

Addressed, period. Angie was probably thinking, *Finally.*

"What do you have in mind?"

Paul looked to Angie. The young woman leaned forward, resting her elbows on the table. "I'd like to keep her in class with me during the lunch hour. She could bring in her lunch, then spend the rest of the time writing."

Mick tapped the table. "Yes, great idea. I mentioned that to her, writing an apology letter to you and the kids in class."

Angie smiled. "Not an apology letter. I'm talking about writing stories."

"Stories?"

"Yes. She's a very talented writer."

Stella did love to write. His daughter never shared with him what she worked on, but she kept a notebook on her nightstand and carried it around the house on weekends, writing in the window seat in the living room, on the deck when the weather was nice, and sometimes in the truck on their way to and from town.

"Are you okay with her spending the lunch hour with me?" Angie asked.

"Of course." He hesitated, looking at each of them. "I'm sorry, but this doesn't sound like much of a punishment."

Angie grinned. "I don't really believe in 'punishment' per se," she said, hooking her fingers in the air. "I think behaviors need to be directed in a positive way. Stella enjoys writing, and from what I've read, it's a healthy outlet for some of her frustrations."

"Frustrations?"

Ben coughed. "Yes, Angie noticed a common theme in what she writes. It's fantasy, but with a lot of family angst. That combined with the acting out might signal some internal stressors."

He must not have hid his shock very well, because Angie's expression was sympathetic.

"Don't be alarmed, Mick," she said. "I do quite a bit of writing myself when I'm not in school. I tend to pick up on that kind of stuff."

"Okay." Mick unclasped his hands and looked down at them. He couldn't help feeling they judged him. Was he not living up to his duties as a father somehow?

"From what I see, Stella isn't causing problems with her peers," added Paul. "This seems to be something she's directing at her teachers."

"And that's a good thing?"

Paul nodded. "I'd rather kids not direct their anger at each other, yes."

Anger? Was Stella angry? A surly preteen, yes, but he never thought she acted out because of some deep-seated anger. Though only four when Raila died, Stella was still very much aware her mother was missing from her life. Once she started school, Stella noticed more than ever the family dynamics of her friends were different from her own. She mentioned it a few times over the years but didn't seem particularly down when she brought up the subject. Being without a mother was simply a fact of Stella's life. Mick wanted to leave the office, to sit in his truck alone and think this through without the three of them studying him, wondering if Stella's home life was stable.

"So I think Angie's idea will help. At the very least, Stella will make a connection with one of her teachers, someone with a common interest. We hope Stella looks to Angie as a mentor of sorts."

Mentor. I hope that's not code for "mother figure."

"Sometimes the transition from fifth to sixth grade is difficult. The kids go from one teacher all day to a new teacher for each subject." He pressed his fingers together, forming a steeple. "They lose their 'mother hen,' so to speak," Ben added.

There we go. Mick shrugged. "It's worth a try." That sounded lame, like he was at the end of his rope with her.

Paul pursed his lips. "There's something else I want to ask you about since you're here."

Again, the steely taste of uncertainly sat at the back of his throat. "What's that?"

"We wondered what's going on with Gretchen signing her out?"

"Stella tells me they go out to lunch, and sometimes Gretchen takes her to work since Stella said she has a light afternoon schedule." Mick shifted in his seat. He'd heard it from Stella, but it wouldn't hurt to check her story. "How often is this happening?"

Paul and Angie looked at each other until Paul spoke up. "Maybe once a week since the beginning of the year?"

A small weight pressed down on Mick's shoulders. "I had no idea it happened that often."

The three of them looked surprised.

"Gretchen doesn't ask your permission?" Ben asked.

Mick rubbed the back of his neck and sighed. He needed to have a talk with Stella's grandmother. "No."

"I know it's a little drastic, but you could adjust the permission form on who's allowed to pick her up."

Mick put his hand up. He didn't want to have that conversation with Gretchen. Not yet anyway. "I'll talk to her."

The meeting wrapped up a few minutes later, leaving Mick to wonder how he'd broach the subject about signing Stella out of school with Gretchen. He hated confrontations. His former mother-in-law wasn't going to take it sitting down. In fact, he'd bet Gretchen would welcome one more reason to dislike him.

Chapter Five

The paddle whirled around the inside of the bowl, mixing the ingredients for blueberry muffins in a nonstop mesmerizing loop. Debi mused about the mixer's sleep-inducing effect. She'd try anything to get to sleep, to *stay* asleep. The pain in her shoulder and upper arm was easing a bit, but not fast enough to suit her. It woke her up in the middle of the night, tight and throbbing if she kept it in one position too long. Maybe Mick Graham was right. Maybe a visit to the doctor was in her future.

She dropped a cup into each space in the muffin tin then slid them into the oven thinking of Mick all the while. The muffins would be a simple "thank you" for taking care of her the other day. It was the least she could do.

Something crinkled in her pocket when Debi wiped her hands on the apron. She pulled out the folded piece of paper. It was the poem from the other day, the one Lon

Holder found underneath the napkin dispenser at his table. She read it silently, smiling to herself.

> *A cup or two of flour and a whole lot of grease*
> *A smattering of sugar, and a sprinkling of yeast*
> *People come from miles around,*
> *To eat these sweets so fair,*
> *There's nothing better with a cup of joe*
> *Than these lovely discs of air.*

Debi laughed out loud, drawing looks from a few customers. Lovely discs of air? She could think of a hundred ways to describe donuts, but "lovely discs of air" wouldn't make the list. Yet it was funny. The poems, silly or serious and most often awkwardly written, always made her smile. Debi wondered if the mysterious poet would ever reveal himself or herself, but then she realized part of the appeal was not knowing.

She stopped the mixer to scrape the sides of the bowl, then turned it on again—only a few more minutes. Debi read the poem again, this time studying the loosely flowing handwriting. Like the other poems, it was written on a half sheet of notebook paper. Whomever left them always did so when the bakery was busiest. And they appeared so infrequently Debi never could piece together any sort of pattern. They were always a nice surprise though, like a bouquet of wildflowers or a stranger's smile. She hung them on the bulletin board, above the counter where customers went for their cream and sugar, alongside the notices of town events, school activities, and small businesses advertising their services. Debi scanned the shop, wondering if her mystery poet was here now.

The door opened to the shop as she tacked the poem onto the bulletin board. It was Donna Marconi, looking years younger than her seventy-plus years. Ever since her health scare last winter, Donna came in for a low-fat treat instead of her usual cinnamon roll. If Debi was the betting type, she'd swear Donna had gone down at least two sizes. Debi could only hope she looked as healthy at seventy. Donna was one of her favorite people.

"Strawberry orange scone today?"

Donna always started at one end of the long case, studying every tray, taking in every sprinkle, as if one certain treat called her name. "I'll take one, and a half-dozen donuts. You pick. My book club ladies aren't fussy," she said, eyes shining from the lighted display.

Debi slid the case door open to fill the pink cardboard box. "What are you reading this month?"

"*The Well of Heavenly Sorrows*. Heard of it?"

Two chocolate glazed rings. Two caramel long johns. Two raspberry-filled bismarcks. And the scone. There. Debi closed the box lid and taped it shut. Pain streaked along her upper arm from the slight movement. She flexed it after she pushed the box toward Donna.

"Nope. Haven't had much time to read lately, let alone go to the library to see what's new."

Donna handed over a ten-dollar bill. "You're too young not to be enjoying yourself."

"I'm enjoying myself. It's not a varied life I lead, but satisfying. For now."

Donna leaned into the counter. "You should talk to Bethany," she whispered. "If you're looking for a night out on the town, I'm sure she'd have someone in mind for you."

Debi couldn't hold back the laugh, turning a few heads with its gusto. She couldn't help herself. Nothing about her was dainty, including her laugh. Why was everyone trying to set her up lately? Did her singleness somehow show on her face? She tucked a stray lock of hair behind her ear, feeling self-conscious.

"A night out on the town in Hendricks isn't exactly enticing. Let's see: there's dinner at Red's. Coffee at Two Tree. And maybe a movie at home if he's tolerable enough to spend another two hours with. Besides, I know everyone here." She might consider a date or two, but anything more felt too serious for someone as independent as herself. Mick Graham was the only tolerable choice that came to mind. He was quiet, kind, and definitely easy to look at. And he had such a close relationship with his daughter—

Debi shook her head. Nope. She was getting ahead of herself. Double nope.

Donna pursed her lips but a smiled lurked behind them. "Just a suggestion. In case that dog of yours wants to get you out of the house."

"Harley is my main man. He's quiet, loyal, and doesn't hog the covers."

"You can't find a man any better than that." Donna winked at her. She looked down at her donut box, pausing. "Maybe you should come to our book club next month."

Debi gestured to the full shop. Every table was filled. "Except I do this while you ladies meet." She might join

Donna and her friends, all retired school teachers, yet they met on Tuesdays for lunch.

"True."

"But thanks for the invite." She noted Donna didn't suggest their meeting time could be changed to accommodate Debi. Not that she expected it. She rubbed her tricep, trying to catch the fleeting shot of pain moving through her arm at random intervals.

"You're also too young for painful limbs. What's up with that arm?"

"I had a little accident the other day." She didn't want to mention the crazy truck driver. She'd get on a roll, complaining. With a busy bakery, there was no telling who might be listening.

"Better get that checked out."

"That has me thinking. You hire someone to help with your beautiful gardens, don't you? I'm looking for a little help in the next few weeks while the arm heals."

"Sure do. My regular guy isn't taking any more business though. He already works twelve-hour days. I can ask him for some names if you'd like."

"That'd be perfect." Debi came around the counter while wiping her hands on her apron before giving Donna a one-armed hug. "Tell Bethany I said hi. Haven't seen her in a few weeks."

"Oh, she's been dating that Nate Ransom fellow since January, and they're always coming and going. I swear she's going to pop in one of these days and announce they've eloped."

Debi liked Bethany. Actually, Bethany might be one of

her favorite people, too, considering she was Donna's granddaughter. They were both cut from the same cloth. Charismatic, life-of-the-party types.

"Really? That serious, huh?"

"Very." Donna rolled her eyes, but she was smiling.

"Excellent. It's about time she found someone good enough for her."

"Someone with a mountain of patience is more like it. That girl can be a pill," said Donna behind her hand before she closed the door behind her.

AT TWO FIFTEEN WHEN THE LAST TWO CUSTOMERS brought their empty mugs to the counter, Debi finished wiping tables and turned the open sign to closed. She grabbed the box of muffins off the back counter, gave a few closing instructions to Holly, then slipped out the back door.

It was a brilliant late-April afternoon, the kind that hurts a person's eyes with the white clean light of midday. She rolled down the window, letting in the cool air, the scents of pine and lake water filling the car. She'd make a point to sit outside with Harley later on, soak up some sun, maybe read one of the many seed catalogs collecting on her desk before it ended up in the recycling bin, unread like the others.

Yes, she had to agree with Donna Marconi. She should probably do a little more playing than she did. Her days consisted of waking, working, eating, then sitting on the couch with Harley at night, binge-watching whatever series some customer recommend she watch. Sundays and

Mondays were her free days. The bakery was open, but Debi let Ronnie and Holly take care of the shop while she caught up with chores around the house. Her calendar wasn't filled with weekend getaways and social events, but she was content. Still, Donna had made her think. Was she missing out on something?

A twinge of guilt pinged her in the chest when she passed her house as she thought of Harley alone. What was she thinking? He was probably sleeping on his back in the middle of her bed, feet in the air. She'd drop the muffins off and be back in a few minutes anyway.

When she got to Mick's place, his truck was gone. Debi pulled into his drive and parked in front of his porch. She sat there for a minute, wondering what to do. She'd had trouble catching her breath on her way out of town, on the way up here to his cabin. Debi figured it was the spring air, heavy with pollen and mold and the dampness from two weeks of almost steady rain that made her breathing uneven. But then she stopped in front of the cabin, in the empty driveway, and sighed. Catching her breath was no trouble now.

Debi remembered the day Mick Graham moved to Hendricks. She'd met him once before, at a Fourth of July party thrown by the Hinsdorff family at their home near Two Rivers. He'd been engaged to Raila Hinsdorff at the time, and they were married six months later. Elaborate wedding, of course. A reception under white tents on the Hinsdorff property. Gretchen arranged for Debi's mother to make the cake. Shortly before their wedding, he'd moved to this cabin. She'd been outside in her yard that day. Debi remembered it so clearly. It was the day Tom first decided he didn't want to be a permanent part of her life anymore. He'd been backing out of their driveway, his pickup loaded with his camping gear and two boxes of clothes, when Mick's U-Haul truck had come rumbling by. Tom was in such a hurry to leave his life behind—leave *her*—that he'd almost broadsided Mick. The near-accident didn't seem to faze Tom, as he was almost out of sight in a matter of seconds, but Mick stopped the truck in the middle of the road. She couldn't imagine what he thought of her standing there, tears staining her face, with her hotheaded husband tearing away from the house like a devil was on his tail. She and Mick exchanged a long look. He asked her if she was okay when he rolled down the window. Debi didn't remember what she said or if she answered him at all. Then he put the truck in gear again and drove away.

Debi came up the steps and set the muffin box on the split log bench beside the door when the thud of footsteps made her stop. Seconds later, the door opened. It was Mick.

She jumped back. "Hi! I didn't think you were here. Your truck. It's—"

"—in town getting work done. I got a ride back from one of the shop guys." Mick stood inside the door, looking out at her.

A strange awkwardness settled between them, Debi on the porch, Mick inside the house staring at her through the screen. Her breath hitched. What now? She was at a loss for words, so she picked up the box.

"I brought these to say thanks for the other day. I'm glad

you and Stella came along after what happened." She tapped the box lid. "Muffins."

"It was nothing," Mick said, raking his fingers through the hair on his forehead. "We couldn't leave you out there, bruised and dripping mud." He stood there behind the screen like she carried some third-world disease.

"Well, thanks anyway." When he didn't move to open the door and take the box from her, Debi set it on the bench again. "I'll just leave them here."

Mick was out the door in an instant. He glanced at the sky, shaking his head in disbelief at some private thought. A short laugh escaped him.

"I'm sorry. You caught me by surprise. I'm being rude again," he said, taking the box.

He was in uniform, the olive shirt and khaki pants, standard dress for the employees of the state park system. The bronze tag on his shirt pocket bore his name and the title of park ranger. In the seconds these few details registered with Debi, that breathing thing happened again, pressing on her lungs, making the air seem like it was in short supply. She laughed too, but it sounded more like Harley's bark instead. *Get a grip on yourself.*

Debi fiddled with one of her hoop earrings until she caught herself. She stuffed her hands in her jacket pocket. "Don't worry about it. It's the middle of the workday. I didn't mean to interrupt."

"Actually, you didn't interrupt. I was about to head outside to meet Stella at the bus stop."

Debi glanced toward the road. "I'd better get going then.

She was upset the other day, seeing me in your wife's shirt. I don't want her to think…anything."

"Anything?"

Debi waved the comment away as she backed toward her car. "Never mind. Enjoy the muffins."

"Wait."

Debi stopped.

Mick walked down the steps from underneath the shadows of his porch and into the sunlight. The breeze ruffled his hair, and Debi noted how the light streaked through his black hair, turning it russet brown on top.

"I didn't say thanks." He shielded his eyes as he looked toward the road. "So…thanks."

"You're welcome." She smiled up at him. "But bringing you muffins was my way of thanking you for the other day. You don't need to thank me for thanking you. Maybe we should—"

Mick put his hand up. "Listen. I'm not very good at this sort of thing," he said while chewing on his lip.

"That's all right. I'm not very good at saying you're welcome either."

"No, that's not it."

Still, he struggled with whatever he tried to say, and Debi looked over her shoulder for the bus again. She really had to get going. Debi shifted her weight onto the other foot, waiting.

Mick frowned. "I think they'll be repaving the road in front of your house soon."

"Excuse me?"

"Potholes. The county has roadwork scheduled for this stretch next month."

"That's great. Thanks for letting me know."

"I'm wondering—"

Brakes squeaked as the bus rolled to a stop behind the break of pines near the road. Debi gripped the car's door handle, ready to duck inside, away from his brooding tween daughter, away from this awkward conversation.

"I need to go. Sorry."

And then she was inside the car, shutting her door before he'd finished his sentence. Mick's expression, as she glanced at him through the windshield, was unreadable. He raised his hand to her. Then a smile dawned on his face as he greeted Stella coming up the drive, and they walked to the porch arm in arm.

Debi didn't miss the dark look Stella gave her when the girl passed by her car. Funny. Apparently, Debi the Donut Lady was a lot less of a threat in the shop than in the Grahams' driveway.

Chapter Six

The parking lot at Red's Tavern was packed a few nights later. Mick parked on the highway and hoofed it across the muddy lot so he wouldn't be late to the dinner meeting. A light drizzle dampened his face as he cut between the vehicles, and if it weren't so cold, a little rain would be tolerable. Inside, he headed for the bar, shucking his wet jacket in the process. He'd need a little something if he had to listen to Gretchen drone on about her newest mining prospect to her guests.

Apparently, he wasn't the only one with that idea. It was three deep in front of the bar before he shouldered his way through to order a draft.

There was a hand on his shoulder and a voice in his ear before he could turn around to see who it was.

"Are you prepared for this rodeo, Mick?"

It was Red Hill, owner of the tavern. He always greeted Mick with a shoulder clap and a tongue-in-cheek comment.

Everyone in town knew Mick and his former mother-in-law didn't see eye to eye. Red liked to rub it in.

Mick let out a short laugh. "Thing is, I like rodeos. I was thinking this would be more like a clown show."

"No kidding. And Gretchen's the ringleader." He looked around, scratching his jaw. "I guess I shouldn't run my mouth since I'm hosting the clown show. I wonder how many digs she'll direct toward you this time?" he said in a low voice.

Mick glanced over Red's shoulder. "Better be careful. No telling who she's got on retainer for being the ears around here."

"I'm not afraid of Gretchen. What's she gonna do to me?"

"Put you out of business maybe? How many of her employees belly up to the bar after work? How many dinners have you served on expense accounts?"

Red's over-confident smile faltered. He craned his neck. "I should probably get back to work. The place is livening up."

Mick pointed to his own forehead. "See that?"

Red looked back at him. "What?"

"It's a bull's-eye for Gretchen. I'll catch you later."

Mick left Red holding his sides, laughing, to go find a seat in the dark-paneled room toward the back of the restaurant, a space reserved for large gatherings. There were a half-dozen round tables covered with red tablecloths and table tents with the Mesabi Holdings logo on it.

Gretchen hosted one of these informational dinners once a year as a goodwill gesture for the city leaders and anyone who had a vested interest in what Mesabi Holdings was doing up there along Lost Pine Road. Since Sheevy's Lake State Park butted up against the mine's property, Mick always had a standing invitation. A free meal in exchange for listening to Gretchen sell the economic virtues of mining iron ore was a small price to pay. Mick would bet most everyone came who got an invite.

Almost all the chairs were taken already, but then he spotted John Billings, one of his part-time rangers, with an empty seat next to him. John waved him over.

"I didn't think many people would make it out tonight with the weather and all." Mick hung his jacket over the back of his chair. Gretchen stood at the podium already, surveying the room. She caught his eye, but her gaze swept over him like he was a dust mote. All the more reason he should take advantage of the free dinner.

John shrugged. "I heard that new prospect up there is a do-or-die thing for the company. Might be only a rumor."

He hadn't heard that. Then again, he wasn't exactly in the loop. Mick had lived in Hendricks for thirteen years, and he was still considered an outsider. It was nothing he aspired to, but he wasn't privy to the gossip like the born-and-raised class in Hendricks. John came from one of those Hendricks families, five generations strong.

As the dinner was served, Gretchen gave her presentation. It was all a big, flashy show, designed to bedazzle the room with her slick technology and big promises. Mick bet half the people in the room had no idea what taconite was or why the stratigraphic dip's angle was important to development. The language they did speak, though, was money, and Gretchen regularly greased the palms of board members on the Broman County Arts Guild, the economic development council, and the park district for their pet projects. A mural installation in city hall—done. A donation for the new visitor's center—they got it. The shelter on the Powder Rock Trail was built in a month from the day it showed up on the city council's meeting agenda. As long as Gretchen handed out money, they didn't mind Mesabi Holdings cutting down large swaths of the forest or blasting dust into the air.

Forty-five minutes later, Mick felt lulled by the prime rib sitting in his stomach and the warm room. Still, Gretchen fielded questions with her frozen smile. He wondered how she held that expression so long. Mick was about to cut out to the restroom when he froze. Someone had asked another question. It wasn't the question that caught him off guard, one about the number of jobs the prospect would generate, but who asked it.

He hadn't even seen Debi across the room; her back was to him with two full tables between them. Now she stood, facing Gretchen, and even from a distance, her anger was on full display in the rigidness of her posture, in the tone of her voice.

John leaned over toward Mick and whispered, "I think this is the first time I've seen Debi at one of these."

"I figured she'd come to all of them. Her property's right next to Gretchen's site up there."

"Not really. Debi's the type to hope for the best until the iron's in the fire," John said. "Besides, she probably doesn't want to stir up trouble. Half the town is in and out of her shop on any given day."

"True."

Gretchen's reply was measured and unemotional. Of course the number of jobs would depend on the size of the prospect, she said. She answered in the most generic way possible. Typical.

Debi spoke again before Gretchen moved on to another question. "And how is the infrastructure going to affect the environment? Already there are tire tracks through my property, and you aren't even mining anything yet. In the grand scheme of things, ruts on private land aren't a big deal. But it shows a careless disregard for other people's property. I'm not convinced it won't get worse."

Gretchen laughed quietly. She put her hand up. "Debi, I understand your concern. Let's get together and talk—"

"Maybe you can answer now? I mean, that's what we're here for, right? To ask questions?"

Several people up front turned around to look at Debi, clearly irritated about her putting Gretchen on the spot by the look of it. Debi noticed, too, but her attention returned to Gretchen, waiting for her to answer.

Gretchen cleared her throat. "It's an important question. No one wants to sacrifice that pristine area up there for industry. And no one certainly wants their property affected—"

"—vandalized." Debi lifted her chin a little higher.

Gretchen glanced to the front table, where her closest allies sat—her foreman, the vice president, the senior geologist. Mick half-expected them to get up and escort

Debi from the room. "By anyone. But there's a bigger payoff, and that's jobs. We both know how important that is to a town like ours."

"I don't think anyone would have the nerve to make Gretchen squirm like that," John whispered. "There's too many people in this room camped out in Gretchen's pocketbook."

Mick breathed deeply through his nose. "You're right. No one wants to jeopardize that."

"But Debi's got a nice little spread up there. It's been in her family a long time," John said, lowering his voice even more. "From what I've heard, the new prospect depends on Gretchen getting that away from her."

Mick leaned back in his chair. "I don't want to be anywhere near that conversation." He didn't know Debi well enough to gauge her reaction to such a proposal, but from what he witnessed tonight, he'd bet Gretchen was in for a fight. Good for Debi, standing up to the powers that be at Mesabi.

Debi wasn't satisfied with Gretchen's answer by her expression. She sat down, disappearing again. Mick leaned forward to see around the crowd, but there were too many people.

Gretchen took another question about the project's timeline, and she was able to end on an upbeat note, everyone laughing at a joke cracked by someone across the room. Still, Mick sensed tension. If what Debi said was true, that trucks regularly ran across her property, she had reason to be upset.

After he said goodbye to John, Mick made his way over

to Debi's table, but the crowd around her was too thick. Someone else caught his attention and he spent the next few minutes talking about plans to restock one of the smaller lakes at the western edge of the park. He'd lost track of time until someone bumped him in the back. He spun around to apologize.

It was Debi. Her face registered the surprise before she smiled up at him, which nearly stopped his breath.

She laid her hand on his forearm "Mick? I didn't know you'd come."

His train of thought crashed when she touched him. "Since the mine is our neighbor, too—"

"Oh, of course." Debi gave him a long look. "You probably have a vested interest in it, what with Gretchen being family."

"She's not really family."

Something in her eyes flickered. Did she not believe him?

"So you're against them expanding the prospect?"

Mick looked around the room. Plenty of people here would be interested in his opinions about mining near Hendricks. For that reason, he steered away from talking about it in public.

"I'd like to talk to you about it, but not here."

Debi narrowed her eyes. "What's wrong with here? I obviously don't care who's listening," she said, chuckling. When he didn't say anything, Debi leaned away from him. "I should be going. I've stirred the pot here long enough. There's a few people I want to catch before they kick me out anyway. See you."

Mick watched Debi weave her way through the crowd again. He got the sense he'd disappointed her. She'd asked him a direct question, and he'd been too worried about who might be listening to give her an honest answer. But he liked her confidence. Actually, he couldn't think of anything he *didn't* like about her. She'd be a formidable foe for Gretchen if his ex-mother-in-law followed through with her plans for Lost Pine Mine.

Chapter Seven

Debi surveyed the terraced garden bed in front of her. Not bad for a morning's work. All of the fall's dead foliage had been pulled, the soil combed over to make way for her seedlings when the frost danger was gone. When Donna Marconi mentioned she knew someone to help Debi with the yard work, Debi never imagined Donna would send a workhorse like Christian Bemmis. The teen barely uttered a word, but Debi couldn't complain. The twenty-dollar bill for two hours worth of work was well worth it. She'd ask Christian to come back next week, too, to help her clear the beds around the house.

As she moved her terra cotta pots from the wheelbarrow to places around the brick patio, her thoughts returned to the other night. Mick surprised her by coming to the meeting, though it made sense he was there. He'd tried talking to her afterward, but she'd shut him down. All she did was ask for his opinion, not to reveal his bank account number. And he'd acted so paranoid. Debi didn't know if she should trust someone so afraid of speaking his mind.

But then Mick had called the next day, asking to stop by her house, and they'd awkwardly sorted out a day and time, stumbling over conflicting calendars and too-long pauses. They'd decided on today.

She turned dirt over in one of the pots with a trowel, thinking. What did he have to say that he couldn't tell her at the meeting or over the phone? Was Gretchen the person he wanted to avoid overhearing him? Maybe there was truth to the rumors they didn't get along.

An engine hummed close by. Debi stood up and looked toward her driveway, at the little cloud of dust raised by whomever turned onto her lane. Mick wasn't due for another hour, yet somehow she knew it was him. Her hand flew to her hair, fingers combing through the tangled mess made by her rosebush thorns picking at her while she cleared away the dried leaves underneath. And her clothes, knees wet with mud, the buttonless flannel covering a tee shirt more brown than white—filthy. There was no time to clean up now. His truck crept up to the house. She felt herself smiling as she walked to meet him.

"Hi there." Debi brushed her hands on her pants. "I'm sorry. I meant to change before you came." She looked at her phone. "I must have gotten the time wrong."

"No, it's me. My schedule was rearranged by someone else today," he said, looking at her from head to toe. He laughed nervously. "No need to change on my account."

Debi glanced down at her dirt-caked clothes and shrugged. "You wanted to talk about the meeting?"

"Sorry for being so—"

"Secretive?" she said with a smile.

"Yes. It wasn't a good idea to talk about it there."

"Sounds serious." Debi wanted to ask him why he cared about who heard him. She didn't mind him coming by though. Debi rarely had visitors to the house.

"You never know who's listening," Mick said. He leaned against his truck.

She was strangely comforted by the interest he took in her well-being this last week. It'd been a long time since she'd been the object of this much attention. That is, aside from satisfying everyone's donut cravings. Her personal life was very much separate from the public profile she maintained at the shop. She liked it that way, but still.

His eyes sharpened. "So the truck incident last week—it wasn't the first time you've had a problem with the mine people, was it?"

"Hardly." She motioned at him to follow her back to the garden.

"I wish they'd been flying down my fork. I could have cited them, driving like that on a park road," he said as he followed close behind.

She thought about saying more, ranting about them running through her property like she did at the meeting, but what for? "I'm not sure it will do any good rehashing it. Besides, I don't even know who it was. What proof do I have?"

"Probably none," he said. "He was going too fast to ID it."

Debi sighed. "Look. I usually keep my mouth shut about

such things. Up until last week, they'd fly on by and I never took it personally." She stopped in front of her garden again.

"And last week was different?"

She gaped at him. "Definitely. They had to swerve to hit that puddle. And I was right next to it."

"I'm sorry. I had to ask since I didn't see it happen. It's not that I don't believe you." Mick massaged his bottom lip between his thumb and forefinger, thinking. "So do you think they're threatening you somehow?"

"Threatening me? He almost ran me over!"

"Sorry. That was a stupid question."

"I don't know what else it could be. Three weeks ago, my mail box was taken out." She knelt down to fill in the hole around the columbine she'd transplanted.

He nodded, now looking at her. "The mine people sometimes think they live in the universe by themselves. Gretchen runs a tight ship."

"Did you come here to defend her?"

"Of course not."

"Are you her spy?" Debi said in a lighthearted tone, but her eyes were serious. "That was the first dinner I've gone to, you know. Ever."

"And why now?"

She tamped down the dirt with her gloved hands then stabbed the trowel into the pot next to her and left it, where it stuck out of the soil like a knife in a victim's back. Debi brushed a stray curl from her forehead. Her hands smelled of dirt and the peppery creeping Charlie she'd pulled from alongside the shed.

"Because Gretchen's prospect is two hundred yards

away, through those trees," she said, pointing north. "Those are my trees. The big ones have been here since my dad's family settled here in the 1853." She looked up at Mick. "I'm not about to let anyone bully this away from me."

Mick swatted at something near his ear, but his gaze didn't leave her face. "I get it. I do. Family's important. Roots are important."

She studied him. "Family history isn't a big deal to everyone, but it is to me." Debi stood up and shook out the stiffness in her knees. "Since my parents moved down south part-time, and my brother and his family settled in Oregon, it's up to me to preserve it. I promised I would." She grabbed the trowel again, working the dirt for no reason other than she felt self-conscious at divulging such intimate thoughts. This wasn't like her, sharing with someone she barely knew. Debi peeled her gardening gloves off and tucked them into her back pocket. "Want to see something cool?"

"Sure."

"Follow me."

They walked around the weather-beaten shed, its hinged door tilted in the frame, and toward the wall of fly honeysuckle standing between the yard and where the forest began. Debi led him around the sleeping remnants of ancient trees, decaying and moss-ridden, and listened to his footballs following her as she brushed aside a blooming shrub as they hiked along the faint path. It was only a few yards in yet hidden from anyone who didn't know what to look for.

Debi stopped. She knelt in the soft underbrush,

sweeping aside the verdant vines that had overtaken the headstone again now that spring arrived. Pockmarked with age, the grave marker was barely legible. Debi watched the etchings fade over the years, rubbed away by the elements, but she knew the name. Asmund Halversen.

"Born in 1837. Is that what it says?" Mick asked, crouching alongside her.

Debi was acutely aware of him beside her, his arm pressed against her hip.

"Yep. A great-great-great-grandfather. Came here from Norway. Logged a lot of the land around here. Built a cabin on the property."

Mick got up and squatted again, a few feet away. Debi watched him push aside more shrubs.

"Here's another."

Debi stood next to him. "There's probably a dozen or so headstones scattered around here. I guess the forest got away from my grandparents when they lived here, and they decided to let nature take over. Part of an iron fence is over there." She pointed off to the right where a mold-mottled obelisk leaned at a tired angle. It could easily be mistaken for another ancient and forlorn stump from a distance.

Mick stood again. He looked around at the forest, a faint smile on his face. "Who knows how many plots like these are in the woods up here."

"That's why Gretchen and her mining ambitions aren't touching one square foot of my property."

He stuffed his hands in his pockets. "When she sets her mind to something, though, watch out."

"Like I said, I've stood my ground this long. No amount

of money could entice me to sell." She watched for his reaction, but Mick showed no expression. Debi wouldn't forget the link between Mick and Gretchen, no matter what she'd heard about how troubled their relationship was. That, and her inclination not to trust easily kept her on guard.

They high-stepped over fallen logs, retracing their steps. Debi almost slipped over a lichen-covered rock, but Mick's arm was around her waist in an instant. She walked the rest of the way through the woods in silence while the feel of his arm against her lingered. The wind picked up, tossing the piles of sodden leaves Debi and Christian raked earlier. It had blown the garden gate open, so she stopped to latch it.

"Look at that."

She pulled her flannel shirt tight around her body and knelt down. The small rosebush she'd planted last fall was uprooted, tossed in the pile of dead foliage. Debi held the mangled canes in her hand. Its roots had been sheared off, probably from Christian's overzealous raking.

Debi held it up. "A casualty of progress."

"It won't make it if you replant?"

She examined the broken, twisted roots. "Nope. It's too distressed." Debi stood, tossing the plant back into the leaf pile.

Minutes later Mick climbed into his truck then rolled down the window. He looked at her, then studied his hands on the steering wheel.

"Do you want to come for dinner sometime?" He lifted his eyes to stare straight ahead at some distant point far away.

He'd blurted it so fast his words tangled together and it took Debi a few extra seconds to decipher what he'd said. When she realized Mick Graham had just asked her for a date, her mouth went dry.

"I don't date."

His eyebrows lifted. Still, he didn't look at her.

"It's only dinner with Stella and me. It's not a date. How about Thursday?"

"I don't know. Stella doesn't seem to like—"

"She's almost a teen. She doesn't like anyone."

"I don't have time. The shop and all. I—"

"You close at two o'clock, right?"

She pressed on the spot underneath her collarbone where her heartbeat skipped. "Well, yes. But there's bookkeeping, and Harley, and I have to be at the shop by four-thirty in the morning, which means I go to bed really early."

"So what time do you eat dinner?" His voice was soft.

Debi inhaled to slow her response. Another excuse sat on the tip of her tongue. He seemed to be having as hard of a time asking as she was finding an excuse.

"Six."

Mick shifted in his seat so he could look at her square. "I can have dinner on the table at six."

Debi shuffled her feet, looking at the ground. She chewed on her lip.

"Is that a yes or no?" Mick asked.

She met his eyes. "Yes."

"Good," he said, his jaw set. "Harley can come too."

"Can I bring anything?"

"Only yourself," he said. "See you Thursday."

As he drove away, Debi wondered what she'd got herself into. Two weeks ago, Mick Graham was just another one of her regular customers. After knowing him for years, never daring to think about him *that* way, or anyone else for that matter, all of the sudden here he was. She puzzled about it as she watched him turn onto High Road, wondering what had changed,

And no, it wasn't only dinner. She smiled to herself as the truck vanished behind the trees.

It was a date.

Chapter Eight

Mick steered the truck around the potholes filled with water on his way up Lost Pine Road to the mine. The sun had finally decided to show after several days of rain. It hadn't been a soaking rain, but a persistent mist, coating the trees with a glossy sheen. When Mick cracked his windows open, enough to let in the crisp April air, the scent of the wet cedar and fir trees filled the inside of the cab. The strains of an old-time country ballad played on the radio, but he'd turned the volume low enough that he could only hear the melody. He needed to relax, to get into a solid frame of mind before he confronted Gretchen. She had a way of unraveling him, though he took pains not to let it show.

He pulled into the puddle-riddled parking lot. Gretchen's car was in its usual spot, underneath the metal carport next to the brick-and-cedar-sided office. Beyond the building, several mining trucks sat near two outbuildings with tires as large as the length of his truck. Mick knew the price of those tires. He could buy himself a new truck with the money one of those cost.

The mine office was empty when he walked inside. Trina Harris, Gretchen's office manager, was nowhere in sight. Then he heard a muffled voice, and when he stepped farther into the room and peered into Gretchen's office, his ex-mother-in-law sat hunched over her desk, her ear to the phone. He took a few steps backward and waited.

If the success of Gretchen's company was written in the materials she used to furnish the room, Mesabi Holdings was a gold mine. The custom-made birchbark base of the front counter showcased the woodworking skill of the guy from Dentsen who did all the high-end cabinetry for wealthy clients from the Twin Cities. A native stone floor and fireplace were pretentious details that gave the impression that no expense had been spared. Her two framed Ansel Adams prints were the only cheap knockoffs Mick could see in the place. He should know; he and Raila bought them as birthday presents for Gretchen the year before Raila died.

"Mick."

Her voice startled Mick. He'd been reading a newspaper article on the wall when she spoke. Gretchen leaned against the door frame of her office when he turned around. She always frowned when she saw him. He'd be suspicious if she stopped.

"Hi, Gretchen."

"I've wanted to talk with you for a while. You saved me a trip to your office."

"Oh?" She never bothered with chitchat either before she jumped to the point.

Gretchen casually picked at one of her nails. "Yes. About that informational meeting last week. I wish I could have caught you before it happened."

"You know where I am." He shrugged. "What does the meeting have to do with me?"

"You're better at those public relations things than I am. I thought maybe for the next one, you could give a little spiel about how this isn't going to affect public lands too much."

Nothing could be further from the truth. He hated public speaking. But that wasn't the reason he would refuse. "You know I can't do that, Gretchen."

"Oh, c'mon. Stop being so pious."

He laughed. "*Pious?* I'd prefer to call it neutral. I'd no sooner speak out against more drilling up here than I'd tell people I'm for it. And besides, it *is* going to affect public lands. A lot."

Gretchen looked at the ceiling. "Truthfully, I expected as much. Never mind." She came around the counter and crossed her arms. Her silver hair, swept into a tidy bun at the base of her neck, lent a stiffness to her movements when she turned her head. "Well, what did you come up here for?"

"It's about Stella."

A flicker of uncertainty crossed her face. Raila had had the same worry wrinkle between her brows. There was a sudden and familiar sadness Mick hadn't felt in ages. Then it passed as quickly as it had come.

"Is she all right?"

"Of course."

Gretchen sighed. "Then what?"

"You signed her out of school last week."

"That is a fact, yes. So?"

"Don't do it anymore without my knowledge."

"I don't think you—"

"I'm not asking you to stop, only to let me know beforehand."

"This is so petty."

"I'm her parent, Gretchen. I can take your name off the contact list at school. Don't make me do that."

She came forward, her heels clicking on the stone tiles. "Listen. I was only going to take her to lunch. But then we got to talking about the new prospect and she was excited. She wanted to see it." Her voice softened like it always did when she felt cornered. It was one of her tactics. "She said she only had technology and study hall after lunch anyway."

"I don't want her missing school. Especially when I don't know about it first. Her teacher says it's been happening on a regular basis."

Gretchen turned her back on him, reaching over the counter for a tabletop calendar. "Then tell me when I can schedule another lunch meeting with her. If you're going to be such a control freak about this, tell me when."

Mick took a deep breath. Control freak. She couldn't be serious.

Her pen hovered over the calendar. She jutted her chin toward him impatiently. "I'm waiting."

"She's twelve. That's a little too young for lunch meetings."

"Not in my book."

"Gretchen. Again, I'm her father. I think I know what's best for her well-being."

"Are you questioning my motives? This is my granddaughter we're talking about, Mick. She's Raila's—my Raila—"

Mick put his hand up to stop her. "I know. I know." Gretchen would be horrified if she knew how well he could read her. The initial confrontation, the wheedling tone, and now the sympathy tactic. He didn't doubt Raila's death had gutted her, but Gretchen wasn't above using it to her gain.

"This is exactly my problem with you. You're an underachiever. You fail to see the opportunity I'm giving her. Stella is showing an *interest* here. This needs to be *cultivated*," she said. "After all, this will be hers someday."

"Underachiever? I'm trying to have a civil conversation, and you have to get personal."

Gretchen waved dismissively. "Don't steer the conversation away from what's important. Stella's the issue, not your feelings."

Their relationship during the last fourteen years had deteriorated from the first day Raila introduced them. Gretchen had told Mick in no uncertain terms he was an unfit partner for her daughter. Since then, Mick kept Gretchen at arm's length. He remembered all too well standing in the background at company gatherings, listening to Gretchen introduce Raila to industry people only to ignore him. Raila was always the one to include him. Maybe he *hadn't* been good enough for Raila. He was independent to a fault, had a tendency to brood, and started too many things he didn't finish. He was also stubborn. That in itself caused he and Gretchen to lock horns over the smallest things. This, however, wasn't a minor issue. Nothing about raising Stella was a minor issue.

"The only thing that needs to be cultivated for now is her education. And it doesn't include bringing her up here during the weekdays."

"If you had a vested interest in what went on here, I bet you wouldn't be so stringent with your rules." She poured herself a cup of coffee and swirled a stirrer around the mug even though she took it black. "This is real-world experience for her."

"Please, Gretchen. That gets so old."

Trina walked in then, unwrapping the scarf from her neck in a rush, glancing nervously at Gretchen.

"Sorry I'm late. There were trucks blocking the road up."

Gretchen sighed loudly. Mick wondered if it was directed at him or Trina for bothering her with trivialities like roadblocks.

"Raila so wanted you to be a part of this. It was important to her."

"I'm doing what I love. I had Raila's full support when I took my job." Mick lowered his voice to spare Trina their drama. Too late. Trina's eyes went wide when he glanced at her. Gretchen's assistant hurried into one of the back offices to escape.

Choosing a life of public service, a government job, with the state parks system when he could have worked for the family business did irreparable harm to his and Gretchen's relationship. If it had been up to Gretchen, he and Raila would have helped manage Mesabi Holdings and overseen Gretchen's prospect network in the Great Lakes region once they graduated college and moved back to Hendricks. As it was, Raila had worked as the company's geologist, forcing Gretchen to hire outside for a second position.

Gretchen shook her head slowly. "Like Raila would have told you if she didn't support it. As strong of a backbone as my daughter had, you were her Achilles heel. No one in their right mind would have turned down the job I offered you."

Mick put his hand on the doorknob. As far as he was concerned, the conversation was over.

"And that you still resent me for it only makes me confident I made the right decision," he said as he opened the door to leave. "Next time you take Stella out of school, I want to know before you do. No exceptions."

Outside, Mick ran his fingers through his hair as walked to his truck. A visit with Gretchen always made him feel unclean. He said things he wouldn't normally say. If she resented him for not working for Mesabi Holdings, he resented *her* for being put in the position. But then he always softened when he thought of Raila. He lost his wife. Gretchen lost her only child. Mick and Gretchen's rocky relationship created a lot of angst for poor Raila. Surely he could let it go for the sake of her memory. He didn't want to linger on his anger. It was possible to push it aside. But with Stella in the middle, with Gretchen playing him against his own daughter, there were no compromises.

Chapter Nine

Two nights later, Debi considered the deja vu moment, standing on Mick's porch with her finger poised at the doorbell. Instead of muffins, she held a raspberry-peach pie this time, and she briefly considered sneaking back to her car. Then she'd drive home so she and Harley could eat the pie themselves without bothering with awkward conversations, surly teenagers, and that weird breathing thing that happened around Mick last time, and was happening again as she stood there. But then her finger seemed to act on its own accord, pressing the bell, and feet scuffed across the floor on the other side before the door opened. Debi didn't expect Stella, but here she was. The girl's small smile made Debi wonder if it was sincere or the result of a father's warning.

"Come in," Stella said, pushing open the screen door a crack before Debi opened it the rest of the way and stepped inside. "My dad is in the kitchen."

"Thank you."

Stella's frozen smile lifted slightly at the corners of her mouth, but no sooner had Debi shut the door behind her then Stella disappeared into another room, a phone at her ear. Debi smiled to herself. She hadn't expected Stella to greet her with the welcome wagon, but she hoped the girl would warm up a little since the last time. Debi had her work cut out for her.

Mick came around the corner, dish towel in hand. "I should have beaten her to the door. She's not the best hostess."

Debi covered her mouth to suppress the laugh that bubbled up. He'd wrapped an apron—cacti and sombreros on a hot pink background—around his waist.

She shook her head. "I'm sorry."

"Apology unnecessary. That's the effect I was going for."

"Congratulations. You got me."

It was the first time she'd really seen him smile, a wide, toothy one. She liked how it lit up his eyes. Mick had pretty dreamy eyes, dark-lashed and soulful, the kind a girl could get lost in. *Careful.*

Mick draped the dish towel over his shoulder. "Besides, I cook better when I wear it."

"I'll have to keep that in mind." Debi offered the pie to him. "For you."

He lifted the pie to smell it. "These sweets. You're going to break my scale."

"*I'm* going to? It's all about pacing yourself. You don't have to eat it all tonight."

His eyes bugged out. "Says the owner of the world's best

donut shop. I can't believe you said that." Mick set the pie on the counter so he could stir something on the stove. "You earn a living by counting on people to NOT control their sweet tooth."

She walked farther into the kitchen and leaned against the island. "That's not fair."

"Have you always wanted to own a donut shop?" he asked over his shoulder.

Debi took a deep breath, exhaling slowly to better control her voice. *Why did people bother with dating if it was this nerve-wracking? She hated the small talk.*

"No. First, I wanted to be a veterinarian. Then I sliced my finger when I was ten. Five stitches later, I decided I didn't like the sight of blood."

"That's kind of a biggie for an aspiring vet."

"Right. Then I wanted to work in a zoo, but the North Shore isn't known for their zoos."

Mick laughed. "That's a problem."

"And around that time my mother bought the shop, so I started working there in high school. I fell in love with making pretty pastries. And I loved watching people's faces when they came up to the case. It never gets old. So I never looked back."

"My opinion might not matter much, but I think it's your gift."

"It matters," she said, noting Mick's profile and how a small smile settled on his lips.

Debi quietly took in the homey kitchen and great room while he was distracted—the honey-hued walls, the vaulted ceilings, the enormous painting by a local artist whose work she recognized hanging above the fireplace. It was warm and unpretentious. On the wall behind her, a framed ornate family tree caught Debi's eye. The generations on the tree traced back to the 1700s. The paper was yellowing, and the calligraphy faded with age too, but it was the gold accents in the flora-and-fauna border that mesmerized her. The detail was stunning. Debi was about to ask Mick about the exquisite heirloom-quality piece when he walked past her, carrying a steaming pot of something delicious smelling on his way to the dining room table.

He raised his eyebrows. "I hope you like curry."

She turned away from the family tree. "I'm game for anything as long as it doesn't involve donuts."

He chuckled. "I imagine not."

Ten minutes later, the rest of dinner was on the table. Stella appeared again and silently took her seat, stealing glances at Debi when she thought Debi didn't notice. Now that Stella sat in front of her, and was too busy gobbling up Mick's curry chicken, Debi stole glimpses of her. She was black-lashed like her father, which emphasized her striking green eyes. A heavy rope of a ponytail fell halfway down her back. Debi could see Mick in her, the dark coloring and slightly pinched nose. Stella hadn't said two words since the three of them sat down. She'd brought a notebook with her, a pen slipped into the wire spiral of its spine, and had set it next to her plate.

"Stella, I see you have a notebook. Do you like to write?" Maybe that would get her talking.

Stella moved to cover the notebook with her hand as if

to sweep it out of sight, but then she stopped. Instead, she shrugged. "Not really."

"Stella," said Mick with a warning tone. "You carry that thing with you everywhere. You're constantly writing when you don't have schoolwork."

"It's not a big deal."

Debi waved it off. "I understand. Didn't mean to pry."

Stella sighed. "Can I be excused?"

The stern look on Mick's face meant otherwise, but he said, "All right."

When Stella was out of earshot, Mick leaned closer. They could touch foreheads if they wanted, and Debi couldn't concentrate on anything else.

"It's her age," he said in a low voice. "She's never been a talker, but getting her to now is worse than going to the dentist."

"I remember that age. It wasn't the greatest. Lots of angst."

"Adolescence is tough for ninety-nine percent of the population, I think. Still, I apologize."

"It doesn't bother me, honestly."

Mick ran his finger around the rim of his water glass. "When her mother died, I worried Stella would be horribly affected by Raila being gone. She'd always been her mother's girl before it happened. With the shock of losing her, Stella became pretty quiet and withdrawn." The corners of his mouth drooped. "But I think kids are resilient like that. Or maybe this is a delayed reaction. She's not exactly a monster, but there's plenty of ornery behind that sweet face."

"She'll be back to normal in a few years." Debi wanted to know more about Raila, but it wasn't a good time. It'd been such a pleasant dinner, and Mick seemed happy. She didn't want to spoil the mood. "At least she didn't refuse to come to the table when she found out I was coming."

His mouth twitched as he continued staring at his glass. "She actually begged to go to a friend's house. But I wasn't about to take her."

"No wonder she didn't talk." She playfully nudged his foot underneath the table, laughing.

Mick sat back in his chair. "Load extra whipped cream and sprinkles on her hot chocolate next time we come in and it'll all be good."

She laughed. A few moments passed between them, his comment hanging in the air. Mick's gaze held hers until her face grew warm and she looked away.

"Well, she seems like a very bright, well-adjusted kid. You're pretty lucky."

"I just wish she'd open up a little more. Get involved at school. She does love writing, even if she acts like she's never picked up a pen before."

"If she's creative, maybe the Arts Guild is worth checking out. They have kids' classes on weekends. I've taken some adult classes myself."

"Painting?" Mick snapped his fingers. "No, let me guess: pottery. You have potter's hands."

Debi chuckled and spread her fingers out before her. "Now I'm wondering what 'potter's hands' look like?"

Mick looked at them too. "Smooth. Strong."

Debi swallowed. "Good guess, but no. Try woodworking, tiling, welding."

"At the Arts Guild?"

Debi nodded. "My home projects border on the weird."

"I'd like to see some of these weird projects the next time I'm over."

Next time. The silence surrounded them. She caught his eye again until her gaze lingered on his smile, which was slow and lazy. Debi wondered how his lips, pink like the inside of a plum, would feel against hers. She blinked to break the spell.

Mick leaned forward again. "I was thinking about our conversation the other day, about your situation with the mine and Gretchen."

"What about it?"

He pushed his chair away from the table so he could stretch his legs. "Has she ever approached you about buying your property?"

"Off and on over the years. Hints and comments when I've run into her. It's never been anything formal, unless she talked with my parents before they moved down south. If she had, they've never mentioned it. But she knows how I feel." She took a sip of her water and studied him. Again, she felt guarded. As much as she liked Mick, she didn't want to give away too much information. She wasn't sure what she told him would stay confidential. "There's no amount of money that would make me sell."

Mick gritted his teeth. "Gretchen can be ruthless when she doesn't get what she wants."

"Ruthless doesn't trump stubborn." Debi rested her elbow on the table and cupped her chin in her hand.

Mick chuckled under his breath. "She still hasn't given up on trying to convince me to support mining over conservation, even after all these years. Gretchen thinks it would be good publicity if she got your local park ranger to okay the cutting down of trees to make way for more drilling."

"So you don't approve? Of mining up here, I mean?"

He hooked his hands behind his head, a move that drew Debi's gaze to the way his sweater stretched across his chest. She quickly looked away, but not before he caught her staring. Mick folded his hands on his stomach as he looked at the ceiling. He seemed to be measuring his words.

"I try to stay neutral for several reasons. People automatically assume that since I work for the park system I'd naturally be on the side of no development," he said, reaching for his water. "I'm a conservationist, true. But I'm not opposed to mining."

Debi chewed on her lip. "I'm not sure I can look at it as objectively as you do when her prospect is in my backyard."

"I don't think I could either, especially with that nice family plot in the woods. That makes the whole idea pretty personal."

She nodded, wishing Mick would take a side, *her* side.

"And then there's always my family ties thrown in to complicate the matter," he said in a hushed tone. "She's got Stella wrapped around her finger, that's for sure, promising the company will be all hers someday. That's a pretty heady proposition for a twelve-year-old."

"I don't envy you. Gretchen isn't the easiest person to know. Can't imagine having a family connection to her." Maybe she could trust him after all. Debi wondered what he would gain by trying to deceive her. Only days ago she'd publicly stated she was opposed to Gretchen developing the Lost Pine Mine site. She wasn't going to hide anything whether he was on her side or not.

Mick rubbed his thighs, sitting up. "Tell you what, this is too dry a topic when there's pie to be eaten."

Debi laughed and the tension in her shoulders melted away. "Show me where you keep the plates and forks. I'll serve."

While Debi cut the pie and served them each a slice on his grandmother's Noritake china, she wondered if almost being pancaked in front of her house might be a mixed blessing. She liked Mick—a lot. It was too early to tell where this was headed, but Debi vowed not to let her heart rule her head. She'd made that mistake before, and it hadn't served her well.

Chapter Ten

Every Saturday morning since Stella was old enough to sit still, Mick took her to the Broman County Library for story hour. First, they'd get breakfast at Debi's Donuts, and afterward they'd walk the block to the library. Mick would sit cross-legged on the primary color rug with little Stella in his lap. A few years later the staff discontinued the program because of lack of interest, but Mick and Stella kept up the Saturday morning routine. After their donut date, the two of them scoured the library for a book or two for the week ahead. Stella loved to sit in one of the overstuffed armchairs near the picture window overlooking Main Street. For an hour or so, they'd read their books together, Stella interrupting Mick to show him an illustration or amaze him with an interesting fact. It was a ritual they'd continued through the years, almost every week without fail.

The head librarian, Betty Gunderschott, had worked for

the library for thirty-seven years. She was soft-spoken with a dry sense of humor and ran the library like she was the CEO of a Fortune 500 company. The library was her world. One time Stella told Mick she thought of Betty as a bonus grandma; the older woman had even come to a few of Stella's birthday parties. Betty was family. So when she asked Mick before Christmas if he would give a presentation on his genealogy research, a hobby he'd picked up after college, Mick could hardly say no. Still, he'd been semi-dreading this Saturday morning for months, and now it was here.

"Do you need anything else, Mick?" Betty asked, adjusting the mic at the podium. She looked over the rims of her glasses at him when he didn't answer right away.

Yes, I'd like to be let off the hook for this presentation.

An older couple walked into the room and took seats in the second row. There were already a dozen people sitting among the six rows of seats. One hundred twenty seats in all. *Please don't let even half that many come.*

"I think I'm set." Mick pulled at his collar. "Is it warm in here, or is it me?"

"I'll adjust the thermostat. And I'll bring you a bottled water in a minute." Betty placed a hand on his arm. "Thank you for coming today."

"I appreciate the invitation, but I hope I don't bore them to tears." Another group of people wandered in and took seats near the front too. If sweat didn't soak his shirt clear down to the hem before this was over, he'd sign up for Toastmasters.

Betty glanced sideways at him and winked. "You'll do fine, Mick. These are all friends of yours."

Was it so obvious he was a nervous wreck?

When Betty left, he paced near the back of the small community room, looking at the one-page outline of his talk in his hand but not comprehending anything. The beige-paneled room did nothing to excite him about giving this presentation. Sure, the research thrilled him, but talking about it to a crowded room? Not so much. Public speaking wasn't on his list of particular talents. His voice tended to get shaky during formal talks, he lost his place on the notecards, and he spent way too much time preparing. Going off on tangents was a given too. He stopped in front of the refreshments table. A pitcher of water sat next to a small stack of Styrofoam cups. He counted the cups—twenty in all. He hoped his audience wouldn't number more than twenty. Yet Mick bet most of the people coming today were his parents' age or older, a forgiving group. And he certainly knew genealogy.

He'd almost talked himself off the ledge when one of Betty's part-time clerks carried in a tray of cookies. Normally he'd count that as a positive, but the person carrying on a very animated conversation with the clerk stopped him cold. His heart plummeted to his heels.

Debi.

Of course she'd come to something like this. He cursed himself for not swiping the flyer for his talk he'd noticed tacked to the bulletin board at the donut shop weeks ago.

"Mick?"

It was Betty again. She handed him a water bottle.

"Are you all right?" she said. "You're looking a little peaked."

More people came into the room. His audience was up to a couple dozen. They'd need more cups.

"Yes, I'm fine." Mick looked at his phone. Five more minutes.

He glanced at Debi again. She hung her head as she ducked into an end seat of one of the rows. Mick thought it funny how she'd try to remain invisible. Debi wasn't someone who could easily blend in, not with that shock of chestnut hair and the whole town knowing her from Debi's Donuts. If only he could fast-forward the day to an hour from now, then this presentation would be history.

"Dad."

Stella poked him in the back at the same time he heard her voice. He turned around.

"What is it?"

"Just wanted to say good luck. And give you this." She handed him a paper.

It was the Robert Burns poem he'd printed off at the last minute before leaving the house. He'd planned to open the talk with it since it was Burns's poetry that inspired Mick to trace his family's Scottish ancestry. He loved how Burns described the landscape of Scotland. He could still picture everything he and Stella experienced on their trip when he read Burns's words.

"Where did you find this?"

"It was inside the book you dumped into the return bin. Colette brought it to me, asking if it was yours."

"Thanks." He folded it and stuck it in his back pocket.

"You're gonna read it, aren't you?"

Mick scrunched up his lips. "Probably not." It didn't feel right now; he'd decided to forget it.

"But you have to. People will laugh at your accent."

"I most definitely did *not* plan to read it with the accent."

She planted her hands on his shoulders and looked at him square. "Dad. If you make them laugh, they'll be more easy on you if you bomb this."

"Gee. Remind me not to confide in you next time." He glanced over her shoulder to the growing audience.

"I know why you're nervous."

Mick growled quietly in the back of his throat. *Not now, Stella.*

"It's because *she's* here."

"You're not helping."

She gave him a cheesy grin and a double thumbs-up as she backed away. "Read it. Trust me."

With Stella safely out of the room—he didn't care if she sat in the lobby since she'd only make faces at him in the audience—he walked to the podium. It was a full house.

His throat tightened. Mick took a deep breath and took the poem from his pocket, unfolding it, focusing on the words that threatened to disappear in a haze of nervous confusion. Betty introduced him, giving a sweet, if somewhat lengthy, list of praise for him as a personal friend and his career accomplishments. Then she stepped to the side of the room, and all eyes were on him.

Mick couldn't look up. Not yet. Not until he'd eased his way through the first few minutes of his talk, when all the words he wanted to say, the notes he'd made to guide his way through this, rearranged themselves into something coherent. It took staring at the notecards, *willing* them to right themselves and make sense again.

Get on with it.

"Thanks for coming today, and thank you, Betty for that humbling introduction." Against the wall, Betty nodded, a worried look wrinkling her brow.

How I wish I were standing over there, and you here.

"Betty asked me to share my journey of tracing one side of my family's history back several centuries, and the tools I used. But first, I'd like to start with the words from a famous Scot. You've probably heard of him." He smoothed the wrinkled paper with Burns's words and started to read, his voice taking on the thick burr of the Scottish dialect:

> *Admiring Nature in her wildest grace,*
> *These northern scenes with weary feet I trace;*
> *O'er many a winding dale and painful steep,*
> *Th' abodes of covey'd grouse and timid sheep—*

He could almost recite it from memory. Mick snuck a look at the people in the front row. Sure enough, they were grinning. *Thanks, Stella. I owe you one.* He kept reading—

> *My savage journey, curious I pursue,*
> *'Till fam'd Breadalbane opens to my view.—*
> *The meeting cliffs each deep-sunk glen divides,*
> *The woods, wild scatter'd, clothe their ample sides—*

When he finished, his voice exhausted from trilling all

those Rs, the room erupted with applause. It put him enough at ease to fumble his way through his outline, and he focused on his slides on the screen behind him instead of the faces before him, especially Debi's. Each time he glanced her way, he lost his train of thought. She hadn't quit grinning since he'd looked up during his reading of Burns. When he stumbled over his words, her smile grew even wider, as if she understood the effect she had on him.

The question-and-answer period lasted longer than he planned. He meant to talk with her, but Debi slipped out of her chair and headed for the door as soon as he wrapped up the main presentation. When he saw her leave, the cloak of self-consciousness lifted from his shoulders and he literally slumped against the podium. Mick cursed himself for being such a weak-kneed idiot. The presence of one person shouldn't affect him that way. Then again, it *was* Debi Thomas. Any red-blooded male would understand the effect.

Chapter Eleven

Debi hurried out of the community room while Mick was still taking questions. The look on his face when she walked in told her he wasn't thrilled she had come. Debi didn't care. Sitting through his forty-five-minute presentation was the perfect excuse to focus on him while he bumbled his way through it. He talked about when he started tracing his family's roots, researching generations on both of his parents' family trees, and his trip to Scotland four years ago. His slideshow of the places he and Stella visited made Debi promise herself she'd look into taking a trip of her own someday. No more *dreaming* of visiting Ireland; she'd start researching tour companies online that night. While he talked, Debi tried her best to blend in yet he sought her face again and again. That kind of attention, even from across the room, made her heartbeat quicken. Debi forced herself to look away, to her hands balled a little too tightly in her lap, to the back of

Henry Callahan's head, to the swirl patterns in the carpet. But his voice drew her back. For some reason, it made her think of stormy days when the thunder rolled through the forest, shaking the walls of her cabin. It was soothing in a wild sort of way.

In the lobby, a book cover on the new releases rack caught her eye and she stopped. Her current book was almost finished. She should check it out. Engrossed in reading the jacket copy, Debi didn't notice who lounged in the upholstered chair not five feet away until she heard her name.

"Hi, Debi."

It was Stella. Her head rested on one of the arms, and she'd draped her legs over the other. An opened book lay across her chest.

Debi stepped away from the bookrack and smiled. "I didn't see you there."

"Obviously," Stella said. Her head cocked to the side, and the pile of raven hair on top of her head shifted. She fought a one-sided smile. "So what did you think of my dad's talk?"

Debi sensed Chip-on-Her-Shoulder Stella was making another appearance by the tone. That was fine. Debi could play it cool too. She shrugged nonchalantly. "It was interesting."

"Only interesting? He'd be hurt if he heard you say that."

"If you think he'd be offended by my word choice, then maybe it should be our little secret. You don't want to see your dad hurt, do you?"

Stella blinked.

"Actually, I'm into ancestry too. Always have been."

The young girl pressed her lips together, giving her a look. "Now you're just saying that because you're scared I'm going to tell him." Stella leaned forward to see inside the community room door. "Isn't he still presenting? Did you seriously leave early?"

Okay, maybe I'm not as smooth as I think.

"He's only taking questions. And I'm in a hurry," she said, checking her phone. "I have an appointment." It was a little white lie as far as Debi was concerned, but Stella didn't need any more ammunition.

Stella squinted at her.

"How come *you're* not in there?" Debi nodded toward the open door. "Shouldn't he be able to count on his daughter at least?" She could throw the banter around too.

Again, Stella gave her a skeptical look. "Nah. He'd rather I read out here. He gets super nervous when people he knows watch him."

"I could tell. Before today I thought he was so low-key."

"He's good at making people think that. Besides, I listened when he practiced at home. It's kind of embarrassing actually. Those pictures of me on the Scotland trip? Yuck. I really didn't want anyone seeing them," she said as she looked out the window. She turned her attention back to Debi. "And when he reads Scottish poetry in what he thinks is a Scottish accent?" Stella rolled her eyes. "Nope, count me out."

"He cracked up the whole room with the accent."

Stella brightened. "That was totally me who suggested it. *Yes!*" she hissed, pumping her arm.

Was this the same uncommunicative teen who sat across from her at dinner the other night?

"Wanna sit down?" Stella lifted her chin toward the empty chair next to her. "That's where my dad usually sits."

Debi looked again at her phone, guilt seeping through her for having to uphold her fake commitment. "I suppose I can for a little bit."

She settled into the chair next to Stella, who sat upright and closed her book. Debi felt drawn to Stella suddenly, like she'd been invited into a secret world where few had been allowed access. And with that realization came a sense she had to drop the pretense.

"So, admission: I haven't always liked the family history stuff. I wanted to live an orphan's life." Debi shrugged, laying her book across her knees. "In fact, I wanted to move to California when I was your age and live in one of those beach caves by myself."

"Whoa. That's intense." Stella let out a short bark. "You didn't like your parents or what?

"My parents were great. *Are* great." Debi cringed at the misstep and paused. "They live part-time in Texas now. I wasn't the best person to be around as a teen."

Stella looked down at her own book and flipped hurriedly through its pages. "My dad says the same thing about me."

"I'm sure he doesn't really think that. People say silly things when they're frustrated."

"Maybe." She looked out the window again. "So when did you decide a beach cave wasn't the best place to run away to?"

Debi sighed. "When my grandma died. I was sixteen. She made the best pies. We stopped selling pies at the shop after she was gone."

"That stinks. I mean about your grandma dying, not that you don't sell pies anymore."

Debi chuckled. "I know what you meant."

Maybe if Debi hadn't been such a surly teen herself, she wouldn't have picked up on what seemed like a subtle shift in Stella's frame of mind. Stella's brows dipped as she picked absentmindedly at the corner of her book.

"Remember when you asked me what I write about the other night?" she asked softly.

"Yes. You didn't want to talk about it."

"No, I didn't. Not with my dad there."

"That's all right. It's not a big deal."

Stella looked at her with those lucid light green eyes. "I write about my mother."

Debi swallowed, nodded. "That's good to write down your feelings."

"It's makes me feel better. You know, about her being gone and stuff."

"Yes, I understand."

"Except sometimes I get tired of writing about it and I just want to talk."

"Do you talk about it with your friends?"

Stella shook her head. "They don't understand. Well, my one friend, Brit, doesn't. It makes her uncomfortable, I think."

Debi folded her hands in her lap, thinking of how to show she cared without coming across as intrusive. She was out of practice at being a confidante. "Maybe you can read to me a little of what you wrote sometime. That is, unless it's private."

"Not really private. My teacher, Mrs. Reil, has read some of my stuff. She says I'm a fantastic writer." She ducked her head, glancing around. "I said that kinda loud."

Debi smiled at the girl's self-effacing nature. "I don't doubt that. Do you let your dad read it?"

Stella shook her head. "Nah. It'd make him sad, I think."

"So you two never talk about your mom?"

"I used to ask about her since I was little when she died. I don't remember her very well. Like just a question here and there. But then I realized he'd always get quiet after I'd brought her up."

"And you didn't want him feeling like that anymore, so you stopped asking."

"That's right." Her backpack sat at her feet and she kicked it lightly. "So I write stuff down. Stories, thoughts."

There was a bit of silence, and Debi figured Stella was done talking. She stood.

"I should probably be going."

Stella looked up at her. That mischievous one-sided smile was back. "It's a good thing you left the talk early."

"Why's that?"

"Because *you* probably make him nervous most of all."

"Oh?"

"Yeah," she said, picking at the corner of her notebook again. "He'd be super mad if he found out I'm telling you this."

"Then why are you?"

"Because he needs to get out more, you know, go on dates or something."

"And you think I can help with that?"

"Sure, why not? He's always liked you." Stella made a face. "I should shut up."

Debi took a step back. "Well…"

Oblivious, Stella went on. "You know how many women who aren't related to us have come to dinner over the years?" She didn't wait for Debi to answer. "One."

It seemed like Stella waited for her to say something, but Debi could only nod.

"Yeah, and that one woman was my third-grade teacher and her husband and kid." Stella laughed, another hoarse bark. "Dad got this weird idea that a teacher appreciation dinner would be fun at the end of the year. Just me, him, and the teacher. You know how long that idea lasted?"

"No idea," Debi croaked.

"One year."

"Why do you think that was?" Debi pressed on the side of her neck where her skin seemed most on fire.

Stella sat back against the chair again. "Because the next year I started acting up. Dad didn't think my teacher would want much to do with me outside her classroom." She gave Debi a self-satisfied smirk. "I was pretty bad."

"I doubt that. Your fourth-grade teacher missed out. And all the others too." Debi winked at her, clutching the book to her chest. "I'll see you around."

Debi checked out the book, then hurried out of the library into the sweet spring air scented with lake water and apple blossoms. Stella's words still echoed in her head. *He's always liked you.*

It had been years since Debi thought about dinner dates and crushes. Too long, maybe. But a bad marriage sometimes does things to a person's head, making the idea of looking for someone special a risk not worth taking. Donuts weren't risky. Follow the recipe and they always came out perfect. And people loved them. Yes, donuts were safe. "More donuts, less dates" would be her motto for the foreseeable future. It would be easy enough to follow if Mick's daughter hadn't put crazy thoughts in her head.

Chapter Twelve

❧❀❧

Mick shoveled the last mound of dirt into the hole around the rosebush and swiped at the sweat trickling down his temple. He glanced over his shoulder at the road, looking for a dust cloud, the telltale sign Debi might be coming up her gravel drive. He'd finish here then wait on her steps with the cooler he'd brought with him.

When he visited the bakery earlier, Mick casually asked Debi about her plans for the day. She was leaving early, she'd said. A doctor's appointment to finally get the shoulder checked out. He hoped she'd come straight home, in time for the lunch he'd bought them, before he had to get back to work. Surely this would be a nice surprise for Debi, right? It'd been a long time since he went out of his way to impress someone. And if she didn't show, he'd leave it on her porch anyway.

After his genealogy presentation last Saturday, he'd

visited Buds n' Blooms to scout around for something to replace her disgraced rosebush. At first he'd studied the varieties of perennials, but the choices overwhelmed him. If he wasn't trying to put too much thought into the plants and their meanings—heather (admiration, *too formal*), hydrangea (heartfelt, *better, but no*), peony (bashful, *not at ALL her*)—he might have had an easier time. But then he came across a nicely shaped rose and settled on the potted plant, his original idea. Its buds were small, not yet opened, but a dusky pink trimmed the edges of one bud. "A pink rose means admiration and poetic romance," the shop owner had told him. He said it'd be perfect, paid for it, then spent the rest of the weekend second-guessing his plan.

Now Mick tamped down the dirt with his boot, careful not to catch his pant legs on the thorny shoots, then rested the shovel on his shoulder as he strode toward his truck. He came around the shed and froze.

"Mick?"

It was Debi. How had he not heard her car pull into the drive?

"Sorry. I had planned to be sitting on your steps when you came home, not skulking around your property."

"Skulking around my property? Is that what this is?" Debi grinned while she noticed the shovel and his shoes with an inch of mud caked on the sides. "What *are* you up to?"

"I'll show you. This way."

Mick led her back the way he'd come, around the shed to the little picket-lined raised bed she'd plant her vegetables in when the frost danger was gone. The newly planted bush now stood guard next to the gate. He gave an exaggerated bow.

"A replacement. For the dead one done in by the Bemmis kid."

"You brought me a rosebush?" Debi asked incredulously.

He couldn't tell if she was happy about it or making fun of him. "Sure. Someone killed your favorite bush."

She bent over to hold one of the delicate buds in between her fingers. "A pink rose. Admiration and joy. Very sweet." Debi wore a languid smile. "I can't help but wonder if donuts have something to do with this?"

He swallowed. She was toying with him, though Mick saw the color creeping up her neck even in the bright light of midday. He wanted to tell her what the store clerk said, that a pink rose meant poetic romance, not joy, but it might embarrass her even more.

"Of course. You make the best donuts on the North Shore."

Debi gave a hearty bellow. "How many times have I heard that before?"

"And this isn't just any rosebush. This is the Stanwell Perpetual rose," he said, pulling the green tag with planting instructions from his shirt pocket. "According to this, it's one of the oldest of heirloom roses."

She took the tag from him. "An heirloom rose. Very appropriate." She cocked her head. "I loved your genealogy talk, by the way."

"Thanks." He shrugged. "I'm not the best speaker."

Debi took her time to respond, poking the grass with the toe of her shoe. "I thought you were a charming speaker."

"You obviously didn't talk to my daughter. She'd already decided I would blow it before I even presented."

Her brow arched. "I did happen to talk to Stella. In the lobby afterward. She scolded me for leaving early."

"Scolded you? I'll have to talk with her."

"No, don't." Debi touched his arm. "She was joking with me. Actually, I was surprised. Totally different kid than the other night at dinner."

His skin burned under her fingers. It took him a few extra seconds to recover. "It—that's the story of my life at the moment. I'm glad you finally saw her charming side."

Debi withdrew her hand. "She also said something that surprised me."

"What's that?" He studied her face when the tone of her voice changed. Their casual talk had turned into something else.

"She said I was the first woman to come to dinner since her third-grade teacher."

Stella *had* changed course, from a teen with a two-word vocabulary to an oversharing matchmaker for her old man. Mick didn't know where this conversation was headed. He also realized Debi didn't seemed fazed by the revelation.

"There's not a lot of opportunity in these parts to meet people. It was probably one of my rare attempts to connect with the community."

"Stella also said—"

"What?"

Debi winced. "Maybe I shouldn't. I think she told me this stuff in confidence."

Mick rocked back on his heels. "Great. Now I've got two

women conspiring against me." He hooked his thumb toward her front porch. "I brought a cooler. Hungry?"

She brightened. "Really? A rosebush *and* lunch? How'd I get so lucky?"

He wondered if she really felt she didn't deserve this. Mick had picked up details over the years about what happened between her and her ex-husband, Tom, who the last Mick heard, was serving time in the Kanabec County jail for stealing a car. His parents were a local family—nice people—but they apparently didn't pass down their pleasant dispositions to their son. Mick had a run-in with him a few years ago at one of the campsites. Tom had brought a raucous group of friends into the park one July weekend, and they'd about broke every one of the park rules during the course of thirty-six hours before Mick told them to leave. The site had been littered with beer cans, food wrappers, and they'd reduced the picnic table to a pile of splintered wood. Mick doused a smoldering fire too, which had been burning in the pit overnight despite the fire danger warnings in the park. Mick had fined him good for that stunt.

They walked back to the house and she led Mick through to her kitchen, a sunny, colorful space overlooking her gardens. Harley bounded down the hallway to launch himself at Mick, all wags and excited yips. Mick knelt down to greet the dog, but Harley was large enough that he knocked Mick back against the counter, body-blocking him like a four-legged linebacker.

"This is some watchdog you have." Mick struggled to

keep Harley from licking his face. Finally, he stood after realizing he wouldn't win that game.

Debi laughed. "Right. Harley would just as soon show you where I keep the valuables if it meant extra snuggles and baby talk." Debi pulled two plates from the cabinet. "But he makes me feel safe since I live here alone. Do you have a dog?"

"We did. A German shepherd, Bella. We had to put her down last year."

Debi gave him a sympathetic look. "I'm sorry."

"It was hard, especially for Stella. She grew up with Bella." Mick lifted the cooler from the floor onto the island in the center of the room. "Someday we'll get another."

He emptied the cooler of the sandwiches, gourmet chips, and fruit salad cups he'd picked up at the Osage Tree Room while he was in town, guessing what Debi might like. He'd become overwhelmed with drink choices for some reason, so by the time he was ready to pay, he'd chosen six bottled sodas and teas.

Her eyes widened when she saw the spread. "I love that place. Thank you. This was so thoughtful of you."

Mick averted his gaze. "I hope you like turkey and cheddar on ciabatta bread, because that's your only choice." His voice cracked. He took a deep breath.

She must have sensed his uncertainty. She reached across the counter and patted his hand. "Mick."

He met her eyes.

"It's been a long time," she said, her voice husky. Her hand had a warm, weighted feel to it. "I'm not used to someone giving me this kind of attention. I hope I don't seem too awkward...or ungrateful."

"You don't." He twisted his hand so his fingers brushed hers before she drew them away. The touch, a whisper of a sensation, coursed through his hand and up his arm and into the back of his throat where it fluttered like the papery wings of a moth before it dissolved.

Debi tucked her hand into the pocket of her sweatshirt. "Truthfully, I'd kind of given up."

The moment hung between them like a saturated cloud. Their eyes locked onto one another's, him mesmerized by the amber starburst in her otherwise blue eyes, until a *thud* interrupted the reverie. Debi startled.

She rushed to the patio door leading to the back deck and peered out. Debi let out a small gasp, then slid open the door, knelt down and picked up the stunned grosbeak lying on its side. Mick watched her massage the bird in her palm, his heart still hammering in his chest. He'd have to take it slow, for both their sakes. The sensation of drifting toward something on the horizon, a place he'd seen only in his dreams, something he'd been desiring for some time, planted itself in his mind. That path, for years crowded with fog, was becoming more visible. Mick looked down at his hands and realized he gripped the edge of the counter so hard his knuckles had turned white. He chuckled to himself, relaxing his hold.

"Poor thing—oh!" Debi lifted her hands. The bird flew off as if the collision with the window never happened.

"Thank goodness. I hate when they don't make it," she said, coming back to the counter. She smiled down at the arrangement of food. "This is wonderful. Did I already say how spoiled I feel?"

Mick smiled, brushing off the twinge of disappointment that their fleeting touch was so short-lived. "Yes, you did. But you can say it again if it makes you happy." His gaze lingered on her face while she sorted the lunch.

As they finished unwrapping the food, Mick noticed a copy of the local Lake Shore Weekly on the counter. It was opened to an article about Blueberry Point Lodge and their new matchmaker weekends for singles. He brought the paper closer.

"Interesting idea. Are you thinking of signing up?" He tapped the article, hoping that wasn't the case.

Debi stopped reading the drink labels to see what he pointed to. She let out a whoop.

"I told Darcy it's not my thing so no, I have no intention of joining a singles weekend. I am providing the baked goods though." She picked up the bottle of cherry cola and unscrewed the cap. She flipped the paper over to the second page of the two-page spread. She pointed to the single column next to the article. "I'm more interested in that than the singles weekend."

Mick saw the poem. It was about water and love and how they shared similar qualities:

> *Life-sustaining, ever-changing,*
> *Raging river, drops aquiver,*
> *An earthly calm,*
> *And heart's true balm,*
> *Like Love,*

Like Water.

"Nice. What about it?"

Debi shrugged. "I like it. It's peaceful and simple." She took a sip of her cola. "Plus, it reminds me of the poems I find at the shop sometimes."

"Someone leaves you poems at work?"

She set the bottle down. "Honestly, I don't know if they're for me. But yes, whoever it is leaves them on napkins, sticky notes, whatever. I tack them up on the bulletin board until I find a new one."

"A secret admirer. A little unnerving."

"I find it charming actually." She looked again at the poem. "This one is by Silas Penn. I Googled him—no luck. Any idea who that might be?"

Mick shrugged. "Nope. Probably some local writer who hides out in a remote cabin all day."

"And gets the town paper to publish his poems when he starts feeling a little too closed off from society. Nice theory," she said with a wink. "Anyway, they appear out of thin air."

Mick chuckled. "And that's not creepy?"

"Not really," she said, smoothing the paper. "They've published several of his poems. I wonder if it's the same person leaving poems at the shop."

"You could always ask at the paper."

"Sometimes I think about popping in there after I leave work, but then I get busy and forget. It's not a big deal," she said, motioning for him to open the deck door while she carried the plates. "I think I'd rather not know. It feels a little Poe-esque, like the mysterious fan who used to leave three roses and a half bottle of cognac on his grave every year on his birthday."

"Except Poe is dead, so he didn't know any better. And it's a role reversal; the writer leaving poems for one of his fans." Mick swung his legs over the picnic bench. "Anyway, I think it's odd."

Debi sat down facing him. She looked at Mick under her lashes, grinning. "Sounds like you're jealous."

Mick huffed and picked up his sandwich. "Hardly. Ghost poets are no competition." It was a joke, but he saw her expression change.

"It also sounds like you're pretty confident of how I feel about you," she said lightheartedly, though her focus was razor-sharp.

The sandwich poised in front of his face, his mouth was open and ready to bite into it. But Mick lowered it, placing it back on the plate. He wanted to take her hand again, and almost reached for it, but second-guessed himself. Instead, he curled his fist, resisting the temptation.

"I have no idea what you think of me. Maybe this is just a friend thing." He could be playful, too, though looking at her, Mick could barely hold the grin on his face without averting his gaze and full-out laughing. His attraction to her must have been so obvious.

Debi's mouth twitched. "Maybe it is, maybe it isn't."

Mick looked down at his hand, laying palm up on the table, and pulled it back. She flirted like she always did with him, like she did with all the other male customers, whether they were twenty-five or sixty-five. Maybe he'd read too far into what he thought were signals. Maybe she didn't want something more. *I'm so out of practice it's pathetic.* "Maybe the plant and this were...too much."

"No, no!" Her brows pinched together. "That's not what I meant at all. See, I can be... awkward. And truthfully"—she looked down and shook her head slightly—"I didn't know what to think when I first saw you here today. My first instinct was to think it was somehow connected with the meeting with...Gretchen."

Of course. He should have thought of that. "You can trust me, Debi."

Her smile faltered while she picked at a corner of her sandwich. Her silence was loud enough that Mick replayed his words, wondering what he'd said to upset her. They ate without talking, instead listening to the *reep-reep-reep* of the nuthatches. A soft breeze massaged the leaves above their heads.

"My ex wasn't the best person," she said finally, still not looking at him. "But I was young and too optimistic for my own good."

"There's nothing wrong with being optimistic."

"There is when you waste too much time thinking a person will change. And sacrificing too much of yourself to prop that person up again and again."

Mick didn't want to share what he knew about Tom. Maybe she knew he was in jail, or maybe she'd stopped keeping track of him. The conversation wasn't about Tom anyway. It was about Debi.

They finished their lunches on the umbrella-covered table while nature kept up its afternoon chorus in the background. Mick liked how the trees crept close to the deck on this side of the house, overtaking what little lawn there was beyond the railing. He would bring his laptop out here every chance he got if this view was his to enjoy.

While Debi gathered their lunch scraps, he sat there a few seconds longer, not wanting to leave, but it was a workday after all. Besides, he wasn't sure Debi wanted him to stay any longer if time weren't an issue. She'd fallen into a contemplative mood. The subject of exes was NOT a talking point during romantic lunches. Mick would add that to the rules he was relearning after all these years alone.

Chapter Thirteen

✻✻✻

Debi brought the tray of sugar cookies to the front of the shop to frost, glancing through the window toward the lake. She couldn't bear to stay in the back to decorate them. It was a beautiful day outside from what she could see, and the windowless kitchen felt like a prison—albeit a sweetly scented one— under the artificial light.

It had been a week since Mick surprised her with lunch and the rosebush, yet Debi still felt as light as one of those whipped cream clouds hanging over the lake. She couldn't remember ever feeling this way, even with Tom. Sure, she'd been crazy-attracted to her ex-husband when she'd spotted him on their first day in the halls of Hendricks High School. She remembered being awed by how tall he'd grown over the summer, how suddenly there were muscles on his lean, tanned arms. It was such a silly thing—teen love—and she wished she hadn't wasted so many years chasing around shallow, empty-headed Tom. But as infatuated as she was with him, he never caused her to pour coffee into her cereal or brush her teeth with hand cream instead of toothpaste. It was Mick's fault she couldn't think straight.

Beside her, Holly filled two boxes of donuts for Darcy at Blueberry Point Lodge. As soon as she finished with the cookies, Debi would deliver them, a perfect excuse to take a ride with her window down. Though only April, summer was in the air.

Debi scooped green frosting into the pastry bag, pushing it toward the tip with her spoon. She massaged the bag, working the thick mixture inside so it came out with a small effort. With her steady hand whirling around the edge of the cookies and the donut shop chatter lulling her, Debi's thoughts settled on Mick again.

She'd spent too much time inside her own head since the day Mick and Stella had picked her up by the side of the road. Something was happening, and she wasn't sure she was ready. During the last twelve years, Debi convinced herself the only person she could count on was herself. Tom had turned her ability to trust inside out. They'd been married two years before Tom decided he didn't like being tied down. She'd spent the better part of eight years trying to work it out with him, falling for empty promises, paying his debts. "Trust me," he said so many times. Debi fell for it repeatedly; she was embarrassed to think of how many times the words worked on her. Then one day they didn't. He'd disappeared for a week, crashed his car, then crawled back to her, asking for a loan. "Trust me," he said when he promised to pay her back by month's end. She learned to say no that day. Finally, she got rid of him and his last name for good two years ago.

Now here was Mick, with his soft-spoken nature and generosity, tempting her to take off the armor. She loved how he stopped whatever he was doing when she spoke to give her undivided attention. She loved his small gifts—the rosebush and the lunch—and his embarrassment at even the slightest fuss on her part. Even his relationship with Stella, the closeness they shared, got her thinking about what-ifs. What if she wasn't too old for marriage and kids? What if Mick was the one?

These thoughts raced through her head as she mindlessly squeezed the icing bag over the cookies, outlining the red iced cookies with a thin green line. She'd add black dots in a minute to mimic watermelon seeds. Three more cookies left.

A sliver of yellow paper caught her eye. One corner of it peeked out from under a pile of old order forms next to the baking sheet. The green piping Debi was so painstakingly adding to the cookies took a zigzagged detour off the edge of the cookie and across several others before she noticed what she was doing. Debi set the bag down and pulled out the paper from under the pile.

Another poem.

Debi waved it in Holly's direction. "Where did this come from?"

"He found it earlier and brought it up to me," said Holly, nodding to the window table.

Lon Holder was at the window table, typing away on his

laptop. He glanced up, hearing his name. When he noticed them looking, he gave a cheerful wave.

Debi tipped her chin at him then spun around, her back to him.

"Why does a poem appear every time he comes in lately?" she whispered.

Holly arced an eyebrow. "Good question."

"I wish I could compare the handwriting." Debi studied the poem. "Wait, you know what? I *am* going to do just that." She pushed away from the counter.

"You're going to do what?" Holly's eyes were as large as dough balls in a vat of hot grease.

"I'm going to demand he show me something with his handwriting on it. I'll watch him write on a napkin. Maybe I'll make him rewrite a line of this poem."

"You're really not going to do that, right?"

"Why not? I'm ready to get to the bottom of this poem mystery."

Holly followed her, looking worried that a scene was about to erupt. "I think it's cool. I like…not knowing who it is."

Debi shrugged, wiping her hands on her apron. "I liked it when it wasn't the same person finding them. It's too much of a coincidence."

The door opened and Stella trounced into the shop with another girl, thin and wide-eyed, trailing behind her.

"Two jelly donuts with powdered sugar, please," Stella said out of breath. "And water too."

Debi crossed her arms, looking at Stella with a sidelong stare.

"Why are you here when I'm pretty sure school is still in session? Does your dad know you're running around town?"

"Kind of. I mean, I *am* in school," she said. Stella's eyes grew large when Debi pursed her lips. "No, really. Our math class came downtown to do an activity at the grocery store. Isn't that right?" She turned to Brit, nodding as if prompting the girl to back her up.

Still skeptical, Debi went behind the counter to get their donuts.

"We should get back," Brit whispered loud enough for Debi to hear.

Debi handed the two girls their donuts then shooed them outside, following them.

"I'll walk with you to the grocery store. I need something for lunch anyway." It was a lie, but with the trouble Mick had keeping Stella in line lately, Debi figured the two-block walk to D & G Grocers would be the least she could do to ensure Stella didn't decide to ditch school.

The sun felt as glorious now as it had looked from inside the bakery all morning. Debi forgot her jacket, but within a minute she hardly felt the effect of the brisk breeze blowing in from the lake since Stella and her friend walked at a good clip.

"Does your teacher even know you left the grocery store?"

Again, Stella's friend made that bug-eyed look when she glanced at her friend. Stella rolled her eyes.

"She won't even notice."

Debi looked straight ahead and said calmly, "So, I guess that's a no."

Stella dug into the donut bag while they walked. She handed Brit hers. "Seriously. She only cares about her pets. I'm not...one of those."

Again, Brit spoke in a hushed tone, but Debi heard her clearly. "That's because you don't care."

"Do too," Stella said with a mouthful of donut, bumping the girl in the shoulder while they walked side by side.

"At least your dad knows math. My parents can't help me at all," Brit said.

Debi smiled at the girls' banter.

"At least your parents give you some space. Mine won't let me talk on the phone without listening in."

Maybe you need to earn back trust for something. That's easier said than done, believe me.

"He can't be that bad, can he?" Debi said it in a joking manner so Stella wouldn't think she was prying.

"My dad is in my face too much. I'm ready for him to have a girlfriend." Stella shot a glance at Debi before she stuffed the rest of the donut in her mouth.

Debi laughed. "Believe it or not, I remember the feeling. I'm not that old to have forgotten how parents tend to be where you don't want them to be, telling you what you don't want to hear."

Stella snorted. "That's exactly right. My dad is like air. He's *everywhere*."

"You're kinda lucky he's involved, though. I imagine it's hard being a single parent."

Stella gave an exaggerated sigh. "But sometimes I just want to be alone, and he doesn't get it." Stella jumped in front of Debi and stopped. "That's why YOU need to help me."

Debi stepped back. "Me?"

"Yes." She put her hands on Debi's shoulders. "It's your turn to have him over for dinner. OR take him to a restaurant. He likes the rib dinner at Red's, by the way—"

Debi giggled.

"I've been trying to set them up," Stella said from the corner of her mouth to Brit, who still wore that wide-eyed expression. Stella looked again at Debi, pressing her palms together. "Please, PLEASE save me."

Debi looked at her shoes, trying to keep the smile off her face. Here was Mick's almost teenaged daughter, whom Debi thought would never warm up to her, suggesting she date her father. Mick would love to hear this.

"I'll do my best. *But* promise me you're not going to ditch class anymore to come to the shop."

"We didn't ditch. You'll see."

The three of them walked into D & G. No one was near the front of the store except for the cashier who stood counting the money in her drawer. She glanced up when Stella burst out laughing after tripping over the doormat.

"See? My teacher didn't even notice," Stella said, spreading her arms wide. She stood on her tiptoes, craning her neck to see over the produce displays to the back of the store. Near the dairy case, a small group of kids and a harried-looking woman with a clipboard stood talking. "She's totally oblivious. Those are the smart kids anyway. That's all she cares about."

Debi looked Stella in the eye. "I'm guessing she cares about kids who want to learn."

Stella clamped her mouth shut. For the first time since she walked into Debi's shop, she didn't have a snappy response.

DEBI MADE SURE STELLA AND HER FRIEND rejoined the group, then she walked back to the shop, loaded the boxes into her car, and headed to Blueberry Point Lodge. During the ten-minute drive to the inn, Debi planned the rest of her day. She'd stop back in town to pick up a few groceries and check out the flats of annuals at Buds N' Blooms for her deck planters. Then she'd take Harley to the Sage River Trail. The day was too beautiful to deny him a romp around the two-mile loop. Maybe she'd asked Mick to join her.

As if on cue, Mick's name showed up on her car's console. She pushed the button for the speaker.

"Hey, I was just thinking of you," she said.

She heard him chuckle. "Same here."

"Which is probably why you called?" she teased. "What's up?"

"I have tickets to a mystery dinner theater in St. Paul in a couple weeks. Do you want to go?"

Sadly, her first instinct was to tell him she'd get back to him. Debi hated that she couldn't jump at the chance for what sounded like a fun time. But her old habit of holing up at home for the weekend by herself was hard to break.

Besides, this was a serious turn. A weekend trip? Was she ready for this?

"I...I'd love to."

"Are you sure?"

The tone of disbelief mixed with pleasure in Mick's voice was unmistakable. Debi smiled in spite of the sudden fluttering in her stomach. "Yes, it sounds fantastic."

"Okay. I've got a call coming in, so I'll talk to you soon."

Debi said goodbye, still smiling to herself as she pulled into the inn's winding gravel drive. She'd think more about this later, to being open to more adventures, to being spontaneous. She wasn't taking a weeks-long vacation with him, for heaven's sake. It was a...an extended date. Yes, that's what it was.

The sandstone building was a Hendricks treasure. Once a private residence, it had operated as an inn for as long as Debi could remember. Now that the Stetmans owned it and used it to lodge some of their tour guests, Darcy managed the venue and had propped it up as a premier destination in the North Shore region.

Darcy and Sean met her when she drove under the porte-cochére and stopped.

"Thanks so much for bringing these out. The day got away from me," said Darcy.

Debi opened her car's hatch. "Not a problem. It's the least I can do for my most steady customer." She looked at Sean, who was ready to bring both boxes inside. "I hear congratulations are in order."

Always short on words, Sean glanced at Darcy before giving her a wide grin. "Thanks."

Darcy handed one of the boxes to Sean. "And I hear congratulations might be in order for you too?"

"Me? I'm not getting married. Or even thinking about it, for that matter."

"No, that's not what I meant. We heard you're selling your house. Hope you're not leaving us."

Debi froze. "Sell my house? Who did you hear that from?"

Darcy glanced to Sean. "You told me, didn't you? Who told you?'

Sean stuffed his hands into his jacket pockets and looked to the ground, thinking. "Who told me that?"

Debi snorted. Who would have started that rumor? "I'm most definitely not selling my house."

Sean snapped his fingers. "John Billings. At the Mesabi Holdings meeting."

John Billings? She had to think for a minute to place the name with a face. Then it came to her. Semi-regular at the shop. Part-time ranger at Sheevy's Lake State Park. He lived in one of the renovated lofts on Rimrock Drive.

Darcy frowned. "I wonder why he thinks that? Did you say something to him he might have misunderstood?"

"I don't think I've said a word to him in months, let alone anything personal, that's for sure." Now she was irritated. John worked with Mick. Maybe Mick said something to give him that impression. She couldn't imagine what, but why else would John Billings pass along that information?

"Well, we're glad it's not true then," Darcy said, laying a

hand on her arm. "I can't imagine you getting rid of the nice spread you have up there."

Debi thanked them and left. That was all she could think about as she drove back into Hendricks and ran her errands. She picked up milk and dog food and stewed about the rumor. She bought a small flat of begonias and geraniums, all the while stewing about the rumor. All the way up High Road, she stewed about the stupid rumor. She'd get to the bottom of it, no doubt about it, but first she had to decide who to confront—John Billings or Mick.

Chapter Fourteen

✦

Bubbles erupted on the surface of the pancakes before Mick flipped them over. He glanced at the clock on the stove. He and Stella had a half hour before they left for school. At the kitchen table, Stella sang off-key to whatever song she listened to on her phone. Mick smiled to himself when she hit an especially ear-splitting note, and she must have heard it despite her earphones since she glanced at him and shot him a sheepish grin.

He set the plate of pancakes in front of her along with a glass bottle of maple syrup he'd bought at the farmer's market last fall. It was the kind that cost three times the amount of the popular brands in the grocery store. Stella insisted on real syrup with her pancakes, one of her new idiosyncrasies that drove him a little crazy. Mick watched her read the label, then give him a little self-satisfied smirk when she caught him looking. He sighed and opened his laptop so he could read his emails before they left the house.

"Debi called while you were in the shower."

He felt his eyes glazing over at the number of emails that had come through since he'd last checked. "Did you answer it?"

Stella snorted. "I never answer your phone."

Mick patted his pants, then checked his shirt pocket, his eyes still on his screen. "Where is it anyway?"

Stella pointed with her fork to the opposite counter.

He gave it a glance. "Don't have time to call her back now. Maybe I'll run by the donut shop after I drop you off," he said to himself. He talked to himself a lot lately. Too much stuff competing for headspace—that was the problem.

Mick's list of emails was endless. Someone wanted him to help coordinate a youth group for the Adopt-a-River program. Last summer's intern needed a letter of reference. Oh, here was a new one: a forwarded message from the Duluth DNR office about some homeowner near Utina Lake claiming "Bigfoot-type prints" walked across wet concrete on his new patio.

"A perfect start to my day," he muttered under his breath as he grabbed a legal pad to jot down the phone number.

"Grandma thinks it's great you and Debi are seeing each other."

That caught his attention. "What?"

"She likes that you're dating again. She said it's about time."

"Did you tell her we're dating? Wait, did I tell *you* we're dating? *I'm* not even sure we are."

"No. She brought it up."

Mick didn't like the sound of that. How would Gretchen have gotten wind of him seeing Debi? It wasn't like they'd been all over town together. And despite what she told Stella, Gretchen was *not* happy he was dating again. In fact, he'd bet Gretchen rarely thought about him outside of seeing him as an obstacle for access to Stella. So the idea that his well-being was important to Gretchen was ludicrous.

He shut his laptop. "And how exactly did my social life come up in the conversation?" He tried to keep his tone light.

Stella sopped up the spot of syrup on her plate with the last forkful of pancake.

"Grandma says Debi's land is important."

Now we were getting somewhere. "Really? Why?"

"Something about it making the prospect more valuable."

"Maybe it is and maybe it isn't, but it's Debi's land, not your grandmother's."

There was an obscene amount of pancake in her mouth, but that didn't stop her from trying to talk around it. "Gwama said—"

He put his hand up. "Chew first."

She rolled her eyes, chewing with exaggerated gusto. Finally, she swallowed. "There. She said everyone has their price."

"I see. So Gretch...your grandmother is going to try to buy Debi's land?"

"Sure," she said with a shrug as if it were as simple as

picking up a jug of milk at the store. "She said she wants to talk to you about it."

Interesting. He was surprised Gretchen would even entertain the idea of speaking to him so soon after their last meeting. But if what Stella said was true, Mick understood why Gretchen might be feeling a little desperate.

LATER THAT AFTERNOON, MICK SAT AT HIS DESK AT the park office, having just finished a phone call with the lead coordinator for the Adopt-a-River group, when Justine Welles, one of his part-time rangers, let out a long, low whistle across the room. She leaned over the desk and peered through the blinds.

"News flash: if you're having a stellar day, it's about to go downhill real fast," she said with a warning look.

Mick crossed the office space to look over Justine's shoulder. Gretchen had pulled into a visitor's spot and stepped out of her car. So Stella was right: Gretchen did want to talk to him. He wasn't counting on it being today.

"Great. Can I sneak out the back door?"

"What?! And leave me to deal with her? No way." Justine huffed and gave him an incredulous look. "What did you do this time?"

Everyone knew of Mick's contentious relationship with Gretchen. It was the butt of a lot of interoffice jokes.

"I can't keep track of all my offenses, but I'm sure it's something I'm not aware of yet." Mick pulled at his shirt collar, which suddenly felt too tight. "I'm going to take her into the conference room."

"Gee, thanks. I was looking forward to some excitement around here."

Mick nodded toward the copier. "There's a handwritten list of group camping permits by the computer to input since the website was down earlier. That's always a good time."

"But I was going to eavesdrop." Justine grinned when he looked her way. "Joking, of course."

A rush of cold air swept in as Gretchen opened the office door. She paused over the threshold, her signature way of getting everyone to stop and take notice. Sadly, it worked. Mick tried it once, at a quarterly meeting with the DNR folks. Someone had asked him if he'd forgotten about the meeting, saying he looked confused at finding the boardroom full of people.

"Hi, Gretchen." Mick smiled, but it felt as insincere as it probably looked.

Gretchen held up a thick file. "Can we talk about something?" she asked Mick before looking pointedly at Justine, the intruder.

Mick held out his arm, ushering her into the conference room. He mouthed "sorry" to Justine before he closed the door behind him.

"I have a favor to ask of you." Gretchen tossed the stack of papers onto the table.

"What are these?" He leafed though the pile. A half-dozen local maps, old ones. Mick recognized some of the names: Yarl Creek, Clearwater Lighthouse, and Tettagouche State Park. Sheevy's Lake and High Road were on the last map. He could point to the exact spot where his house sat, years before it was built. This particular map showed the geological features of the area.

Gretchen picked that map out of the pile. "This one is actually the most interesting to me." She pointed to a spot in the upper right-hand corner. "See that? That's my Lost Pine Mine prospect there."

Mick crossed his arms. "Yes, there it is. How does this involve me?"

"You're so impatient. Why can't we have a normal conversation without all the animosity?"

This diplomatic approach was new. She must be desperate.

"I'm at work, Gretchen. Whatever this is, I'm not sure why you had to come in the middle of the day. You could have waited until I was at home."

She pressed her fingers into the sides of her temples, speaking with clipped words. "I need your expertise, and I need it fast."

Mick pulled out a chair. "Let's slow down a minute. Sit down." He waited until she was seated before he planted himself opposite her across the table.

"Now, what is so important that it needs my immediate attention?"

"I've heard from someone connected to Consolidated Iron. It's hearsay at this point, but this person says they won't buy the prospect from me unless I can acquire this section right here." She tapped the area near High Road. It was 640 acres of the partially forested land next to property owned by Gretchen's company. It was the land that had been in Debi's family for generations.

Gretchen continued. "The area butting up against my property has the purest ore in all of what I own up there. Raila's research says so."

Mick remembered Raila working on those reports ten years ago. It had been part of her master's thesis research. Mick knew exactly how valuable that land might be to Mesabi Holdings if Gretchen was in the business of selling it to a larger company.

He sighed. "What do you want me to do?"

She planted her elbows on the table, folding her hands under her chin. "I want you to review these maps for me and help prepare a new report, focusing on the land south of my prospect."

"But you don't own that land. It's Debi Thomas's property."

"I'm negotiating with her to buy it."

"Really?" He rubbed his jaw, thinking.

After listening to Debi's direct questions at the Mesabi-sponsored dinner last week, and then the passionate, anger-infused words she'd used when he'd stopped by her house, he couldn't imagine Debi changing her mind so quickly. Maybe what Gretchen said to Stella was the truth. Maybe everyone did have a price.

"I expect we'll settle on the terms within the next week. This is all very unofficial yet, so I'd appreciate your discretion."

Why hadn't Debi told him she was considering the sale? Did she not trust him because of his association with his ex-mother-in-law?

"You know I can't rework these maps, Gretchen."

She froze. "Why on earth not?"

"It's a conflict of interest."

"These maps represent years of Raila's research. You most certainly can work with this data. You owe it to her. She would want you to help me."

Mick sighed, leaning back in his chair. "Why doesn't your geologist prepare this for you?"

"*You're* a geologist."

"Not this kind of geologist. You referred to me as 'just a park ranger' when I decided to take the Sheevy's Lake job instead of work for you anyway. Remember that?"

"I was hurt," she said, that wheedling tone creeping into her voice. "I had high hopes for you and Raila taking over the company someday." She waved the thought away. "Water under the bridge, as they say. If this acquisition goes through, I'll have no problem selling the prospect up there. And I think you know what that means for Stella. She'll have a nice nest egg when I decide to hand over the reins."

Mick didn't want to start an argument in the office. Standing, he'd heard enough.

Gretchen drummed her fingers on the table. "What, you don't like the idea of Stella running the company? Think about her future, Mick."

"I think we're finished here. I need to get back to work."

"She looks up to me as a role model, you know."

Mick lifted his brows, avoiding her gaze. *Don't say a thing.*

"She confides in me. And here's something you may not know: She's not crazy about Debi hanging around. She doesn't feel like she can talk to you about it though."

That wasn't the impression Stella gave him. If anything,

his daughter seemed thrilled her instincts about Mick being interested in Debi were true.

"Outside of Stella, my personal life is absolutely none of your business."

"What am I supposed to do? Tell Stella she shouldn't talk to me?"

Mick inhaled deeply. Once again Gretchen was trying to meddle in his life. He didn't doubt she loved Stella, yet Gretchen's motives never felt genuine. She thrived on trying to control things she had no business being involved in. And Gretchen was not above using Stella as a wedge between him and his daughter.

He'd vowed years ago to keep his opinions about developing the land near Hendricks to himself. As a conservationist for the DNR, who also happened to have a personal connection to the largest mining operation in the area, it was important to stay neutral. He didn't want to take sides, especially since he lived in the community where he also worked. And now with Debi's property suddenly at the center, thanks to Gretchen, keeping his opinion to himself was more important than ever.

Gretchen gathered the maps on the table. "I'll send you an email with the details in case you change your mind. You need to do this for Raila and Stella if you're too selfish to do it to help me."

He walked Gretchen to the door, opening it to hurry her along. "I won't change my mind, but I know that won't stop you."

Chapter Fifteen

Debi latched the shed's door after dumping her potting tools inside. Harley rummaged around the foundation, probably catching the scent of the red fox family Debi spotted playing together on mornings during the last few weeks. There was a burrow underneath the shed, fresh dirt kicked around the hole, and a space large enough for an animal to squeeze into for shelter. Debi called off Harley, and he usually listened well, but he'd grown bored watching her transplant annuals for two hours and didn't even pause. He kicked back more dirt like a four-legged backhoe. Harley had an agenda.

"Harley, let's go."

When the dog stayed put, rump in the air, tail waving like a metronome, Debi gripped him by the hindquarters and pulled him out.

"I'm going to get your leash if you don't listen."

He looked at her with indifference before his ears perked

up and he took off toward the woods. Debi sighed. Nothing held his attention for long.

At least a calm had settled over her since leaving Blueberry Point Lodge now that her hands were dirty. Gardening did that for her. It was one of those mindless jobs, like frosting cookies, that allowed her thoughts to wander. It still irritated her that someone fabricated a rumor about her selling. Then Debi shook her head. *Stop, please. You'll get worked up again.*

Shadows crept across the yard as the sun dipped farther into the horizon behind the trees. She loved spring when the earth came alive with color, like the white stars of wild geraniums and the honeysuckle, ever-twining its woody vines around anything in its path. Debi gave it props for its luscious berry-hued blossoms. There couldn't be enough flowers to suit her.

Up ahead, Harley leapt into undergrowth near the stand of purple-stemmed asters that separated her lawn from the wild growth of the forest. She followed him as he headed toward the headstones. The path, worn from decades of Thomas family members trodding through the woods to the plot, was still visible. Soon it would be swallowed in a wild green blanket.

She knelt down near the first headstone she came to, pushing away the new growth, pulling some weeds from its base. She'd fight it all summer long, the weeds and vines trying to lay claim to the slabs and her refusing to let Mother Nature win. The cool stone underneath her fingertips soothed her. She traced the numbers "1874" with her finger, feeling how the elements had smoothed the harsh edges made by a chisel so long ago. Someday the numbers would fade like the name above it had already. Debi meant to buy a cake of rubbing wax and some white interface to preserve the etchings, but it never seemed to move up on her to-do list.

Harley barked. Debi looked up, but he'd disappeared in the brush. He'd need a bath after digging under the shed and who knew what else he'd got into now. She stood up and tried to track him, but the shadows were getting longer and his bark sounded too distant.

She'd buy the wax cake and interface tomorrow now that she finished with the mudroom floor. That had been a big project—adhering hundreds of bottle caps to the concrete before pouring a thick coat of epoxy for a sealant. *You did what?* her mother asked incredulously over the phone yesterday when Debi told her. The floor was as smooth as glass, Debi reassured her. Admittedly, some of Debi's home projects bordered on the weird, but the bottle cap floor had turned out amazingly well.

During the years she'd struggled to make sense of her crumbling marriage, Debi made an effort to focus on what made her happy. She'd become an expert at switching off the stressors that might have driven her mad if she let them take hold, and instead cultivated her love of gardening and art. Handmakery Folk Art Studio was her favorite place early on, second only to the sanctuary of her home. The owner, Letta Arbuckle, had taken Debi under her creative wings, opening the studio to her 24/7 if she needed, which was often when Tom started drinking. Debi's loom projects and watercolor landscapes transitioned to woodcarving and furniture refinishing. She'd become pretty good at the home improvement projects too. She loved the whimsical—a quotation inked onto the window frame in her bedroom, a hand-painted tile added to the sterile taupe backsplash in the kitchen. The bottle cap floor was her most quirky project yet. She adored it.

Debi pulled one last clump of vines from the ground, adding it to the fistful she had gathered, and scanned the area for her crazy dog.

She froze.

The hair on her neck prickled.

Someone was watching her.

The sensation slithered over her psyche, goosebumps crawling down her arms. Most of the trees in this part of her woods were saplings, crowded in the understory of the larger cedars, birches, and firs. Still, there were plenty of trees with a wide enough girth to hide a man.

"Harley, come!"

To her right, something shifted in her peripheral vision. Debi's eyes darted in that direction, studying the trees. Nothing.

It could be an animal. But it wasn't; she was sure of it. It was too big, too fluid. She knew that as well as she knew her own name.

Debi retraced her steps, walking backward and tripping, slowly planting her feet, trying to look everywhere at once. She didn't want to turn her back just yet. Not until she was closer to the house.

Harley's throaty growl sounded close by.

"Harley!"

A shush of vegetation startled Debi before Harley bounded out. His tongue lolled to one side. He'd obviously been romping, his panting labored and uneven. Harley's triangular ears perked, and he stopped to look behind him. Then he bounded ahead a few yards, froze, and looked again toward the woods. When Debi caught up to him, she grabbed him by the collar—he wouldn't desert her again—and hurried out of the woods.

Once inside, Debi locked her door and went from room to room, drawing the shades while her pulse beat in her ears. She left the lights off and stopped in the spare bedroom to peer from behind the blinds, separating slats with her fingers ever so slightly to peer outside. Nothing.

Only then did she reach for her phone in her pocket. She punched in Mick's number while she settled on her bed in the other room, in the only room without windows facing the forest.

"Mick, can you come over? There's someone in the woods."

Chapter Sixteen

✥

Mick heard the panic in Debi's voice even before he made sense of why she called. He'd known Debi long enough to realize she wasn't prone to theatrics. Eight minutes later, he pulled in front of her house. The sun had dipped far enough behind the trees that last light was only minutes away. It wouldn't do any good to stomp around in the woods with a flashlight at this point. If anyone had been out there, Mick bet they were long gone.

There was a wild look in Debi's eyes when she let him in the house.

"Thank you so much for coming. I never saw anyone, but I sensed it, and Harley reacted too."

Mick shrugged off his jacket as they went into her kitchen. He settled on a stool. "Maybe it was a deer. Or campers out for a walk?"

"I've had plenty of deer watch me from the woods. They don't spook me. There was someone out there. And why would campers be this far off the trails? On this side of High Road no less?"

"It happens more often than you think."

Debi's face faltered. "So you think I'm being paranoid?"

"No, I'm not saying that at all."

She sighed. "I *hate* feeling vulnerable. It makes me feel weak. I don't have time for this."

Mick smiled. "You're hardly weak."

Debi sighed again. "You're right." She shook out her arms. "I hope it's not related to, you know, the truck incident. If it's someone from the mine, they'll find out who they're messing with in a real hurry. I'm tired of this." Debi knocked her fists together and tried to keep from smiling.

Mick stood, taking her hands in his. "They won't. Not anymore," he whispered, drawing her close.

She drew back. "Anymore? What does that mean?"

"You called them out on it at the meeting. If anything was going on, you put a stop to it. That's all I meant."

"You're right." She sighed and slipped her hands away from his. "I'm sorry. This really irritates me. Someone's invaded my privacy."

"Let's sit. You're still worked up." Mick took her by the hand again and led her to the couch. "I'll make you some tea."

He found tea bags on the counter but fumbled around the unfamiliar kitchen looking for a mug and a spoon. On the couch, Debi leaned her head back, closing her eyes.

"So, you seem to be awfully suspicious of Gretchen and her people." He filled the mug with water and set it in the microwave to heat. "I mean, the guy in the truck was an idiot, but are you sure it wasn't just an accident?"

"I can't even count the times I've had problems with them."

"When was the last time you talked to Gretchen?"

"I can't even remember. Years."

"And what was the gist of the conversation then?"

Debi opened her eyes, still looking at the ceiling. "She made demands. I told her to get lost."

"I'm sure that went over well." He gritted his teeth.

"There were, ah...choice words."

He handed her the steaming mug. "Here you go."

"Thank you."

Mick sat across from her, and Harley took that as an invitation to lay his head across Mick's knee. When he didn't acknowledge the dog right away, Harley nosed Mick's hand.

Debi lifted the mug to blow on it and giggled. "Warning: He's not subtle."

Mick scratched Harley under his chin. "I'm not a fan of beating around the bush either."

Their eyes locked for a prolonged moment. Her face was still flush from being outside. It enhanced the blueness of her eyes. Their lips were so close, only inches from touching, tasting.

Mick's hand slid up the length of her arm, his fingers grazing a lock of hair falling onto her shoulder, then to her neck, and she leaned toward him and...a kiss. Its softness made the room seem to waver before he closed his eyes. A sweetness brushed Mick's throat as he inhaled, the tea still moistening her lips, tasting of lavender. The urgency nearly made him see stars. Then it was over much too soon for his liking.

Debi looked down at the mug in her lap. A wet spot dampened the knee of her jeans where the tea had sloshed over the side. She set it on the table and let out a soft laugh. Maybe she was as surprised as he was about the kiss. Debi placed a hand on his knee when she looked up at him.

"I need to ask you something, but it's awkward."

She hadn't even asked yet but already he felt guilty of something underneath her scrutiny. Her hand on his knee, though. He couldn't look away from it.

"What is it?"

"I took a delivery to Blueberry Point Lodge earlier today and heard a weird rumor."

"A rumor about what?"

"Sean Stetman said he heard from John Billings that I'm selling my property."

He felt his face flush. "What? Where would he get that idea?"

"That was exactly my question. Sean said John mentioned it to him at the Mesabi Holdings meeting. Weren't you with him that night?"

Mick got up to get her a towel for the spilled tea. He handed her the towel then sat opposite her. "Yes, I saw him there. We sat together."

"And did he mention anything to you? I'm just trying to figure out where this came from."

"He didn't get it from me." Mick didn't think she

accused him, but he couldn't help feeling a little defensive. "I wouldn't talk about your personal business with anyone."

"No, I didn't think you would." She pressed her lips together, irritated.

"I can ask John about it. He'd be discreet. He'd tell me the truth."

Debi rested her elbows on her knees and stared at the floor. "I'm sorry. I can't help but think whoever was lurking in my woods is another one of Gretchen's people trying to intimidate me. Like the guy in the truck. Like all of the wicked looks I got from her top managers at the meeting."

When he didn't say anything, Debi looked up. "I know you don't think so, but that's how I feel."

Mick got up to sit next to her and put his arm around her shoulders. She leaned against him, resting her head against his. He breathed in the scent of her hair. Mick didn't want to take advantage of the situation, but he couldn't help the wave of desire that came over him.

"I don't know who was out there or why, but I don't think you have to worry."

She looked up at him. "Why do you think that?"

He hugged her tighter. "Gretchen isn't the nicest person, but I just don't think she'd send someone out to your woods to scare you. That's not her game."

Debi gave him a look, one brow arching. "Really?"

"Yes. She doesn't want the town thinking her company promotes thug tactics. If I know her as well as I think I do, she takes pride in influencing people. She'd much rather get you into a conference room and try to negotiate than send someone to trespass on your property."

"I hope you're right."

"Trust me."

Debi stiffened. She looked over his shoulder, but Mick saw her eyebrows pinch.

He drew his arms back. "What's wrong?"

Her smile wavered. "What you...said just now. Tom asked me to trust him all the time."

"Debi, I didn't—"

She waved her hand. "Don't worry about it. It's just me."

Mick swallowed, afraid to say anything more. She was right, though. It was her trigger. Had he known, Mick never would have uttered those words.

She took her mug to the kitchen, and Mick watched her pause in front of the window, staring out at the dark forest, her reflection in the glass. "I'll be okay. I've got Harley here anyway."

That was a dismissal if Mick ever heard one. "Are you sure? I can...stay on the couch. Or I'll sleep in my truck, if you'd rather."

Debi whooped at that, the first real display of humor she'd shown since he'd come over. "Don't be silly. You need to worry about Stella more than me anyway." She turned toward him and her expression softened. "You're right, Mick. I can't help being paranoid."

"I didn't say you were paranoid."

"No, I guess you didn't."

Mick didn't like the tone the conversation had taken. If he left now, it couldn't deteriorate any further. "I'll check with you in the morning then. See how you're doing."

Debi pulled her sweater around her neck. "Yes, that'd be perfect."

Outside, he sat in his truck for a minute, listening to the engine rumble, while wishing for a redo of their conversation.

Trust me.

Mick cursed himself for saying it. He'd catch himself next time.

Chapter Seventeen

❧

For everything moving in the right direction with Mick, Debi couldn't help but wonder if the opposite were true at the shop.

She sat at one of the tables, filling napkins dispensers the next Wednesday morning. It was a few minutes after eight o'clock, yet there was no line to the door, the coffee carafe was still filled with the first brew, and the donut case was almost fully stocked. The place usually buzzed with coffee-fueled conversation at this hour. It had been nearly empty last week too. Something was up.

Her regular groups like the card-playing retirees who came in most mornings between seven and eight o'clock and shared a carafe while they played canasta still arrived with faithful regularity. And Red and Tonti Hill popped in for their decafs and glazed rings every day too. Yet, the mining group's absence was the most obvious. They were usually the loudest, most raucous bunch, and while she didn't miss the commotion, the donut trays didn't empty as fast since they'd stopped coming.

It was so quiet Debi heard the timer ticking away in the back, counting down the minutes until the scones were done.

Behind the counter, Holly screwed the top onto a yellow pitcher. "What's up with this? I've never seen it empty at this hour."

"Strange, isn't it? Did a new bakery open up in town and we're the last to know?"

Holly came from behind the counter with the pitcher to water the spider plant hanging near the front window.

"Even if one did, you wouldn't have to worry. This is the world's best donut shop. No competition."

"Thank you for saying so." Debi stuffed napkins into the container. "Well, the mine guys haven't been coming in. That makes a big difference. I wonder why?"

Holly shrugged, but Debi noticed how she averted her eyes.

"Holly, you know something, don't you?"

The young girl groaned. "I hate that my face can never keep secrets."

Debi couldn't help but laugh. "Secrets? What did I miss?"

Setting the watering can behind the counter, Holly came over and sat down opposite Debi. She crossed her arms.

"It's not a secret. I mean, no one said, 'Holly, promise not to tell Debi.' But I heard some people talking in here the other day, about how your questions at the Mesabi Holdings dinner were...anti-mining."

"*Anti-mining?* I spoke up because their decisions could affect my life." Debi crammed more napkins into the dispenser. That figured. Leave it to the Lost Pine Mine people to not understand why she'd ask those questions. They acted as if they were the only ones in the world. She couldn't care less if they developed their prospect up near High Road as long as they stayed far away from her property.

"I'm sorry. I didn't mean to bring it up." Holly folded her hands together on the tabletop.

Debi slumped but laid a hand on Holly's. "No, don't worry about it. I asked."

The door chimes fluttered. Debi stuffed the last of the napkins into the dispenser and glanced up.

Lon Holder.

He looked…different. Maybe he was a little more closely shaven. Or maybe it was the blue blazer he wore over his customary short-sleeved polo. Whatever it was made Debi do a double take. She might even venture to say he was good-looking. Maybe it was her imagination, but his face lit up when he saw her too.

Lon made a show of looking around at the empty tables. "Are there rumors circulating about cockroaches in the cupcakes?"

Okay, maybe he wasn't so handsome.

Debi exchanged looks with Holly. The young girl's mouth hung open ever so slightly.

"No." Debi stood up. Did he really just say that to her? She thought he was so pleasant the last time he came in.

"Centipedes in the scones?"

Not one iota of handsome. There was no use fighting the scowl that pinched her eyebrows together. Good riddance if she lost his business.

"Did you come in here to make my day worse or place an order?"

Lon looked shocked. "I thought I was being witty."

"If that's what you call witty, I'd hate to hear your insults."

He winced. "I'm sorry. Maybe I should just order."

"Great idea."

Debi got him his coffee and a chocolate frosted bismarck. While he stirred creamer into his mug, he paused.

"I didn't mean to sound like such a jerk. The empty shop surprised me is all."

"You and me both." Debi wiped her finger smudged with chocolate onto her apron and waved dismissively. "I'm over it."

His expression changed momentarily when she said that. Did he look sympathetic? It was such a fleeting look, but then he went to sit at his usual table and Debi got a roll of paper towels and a rag to wipe the cases down.

If she stewed about missing the Lost Pine Mine employees earlier, she was finished now. Debi wouldn't sweat their absence if it meant she couldn't speak her mind at a public meeting. How dare they spread rumors and boycott her for voicing her opinion. Lon's supposedly innocent remarks sealed her resolve. The health department would probably show up in the next week, thanks to him. He'd claim it was all a joke, of course. Cockroaches in the cupcakes—*humph*. No, thanks. She'd find another way to make up for the loss of their business.

Debi was about to close the door on the first case when she spotted Lon's legs through the Plexiglass window. *What did he want now?*

"Found this," he said, handing her the familiar half sheet of lined yellow paper folded into a two-inch square.

Her heart lifted in a rush. Another poem.

"Where?"

"Under my napkin dispenser. Who is this person?" Lon squinted at her. "Secret admirer?"

She'd filled the dispensers at almost all the tables, though now that she thought about it, all of them except the window table. Debi unfolded the paper.

I am more than sodden leaves, fallen limbs,
And the soil sifting between your fingers.
I am a legacy of memories,
A lifeline, and more.
The earth knows its worth.
Do you?

It was signed, *Silas Penn.*

Debi let out a little gasp. She read the poem again, lingering on the question at the end. This had been written for *her*. And it had been signed—a first! She'd noticed the similarities between the Silas Penn poems published in the newspaper and those she found in her shop. But she'd never been able to officially link them since her donut shop poet hadn't included a name until today. *Why now?*

During the next half hour, Lon sat at the window table and worked on his laptop. Debi watched him off and on while she cleaned the cases. He stole glances at her until she looked up and caught him outright staring at her. Would he pull a napkin from the dispenser and scribble down a poem? Did he have lined paper in his leather bag to fill up with words if he was inspired? She never thought Lon might be her secret admirer, but now that she studied the coincidences, *yes*, it could be Lon. The longer she watched him, the more sure she was that he was the culprit. But the possibility of her returning his affections? *That* was as remote as her craving a sugarless donut.

As Debi turned this scenario over in her mind, Lon reached into his briefcase and pulled out a legal pad—yellow paper!—and she gasped again.

Holly poked her head out of the back room, a frosting piping bag in one hand.

"You all right?"

Debi waved her off. "Yes. Sorry. Thought I forgot an appointment, but I've got my days mixed up."

Holly gave her a skeptical look and disappeared.

Debi stood at the counter, tapping her blue fingernails on the laminate surface. The suspense would give her an anxiety attack if she didn't do something about it. The time to confront him was now, even if it was against her better judgment. Debi tossed the rag over her shoulder and marched to his table.

"Excuse me."

Lon looked up at her.

"This is really awkward but—"

That same smug grin crinkled his eyes at the corners in a not-too-awful way. "What is it?"

She didn't know how to ask him if he was the mysterious Silas Penn. Should she come right out and mention her suspicion? What if he said no? That would definitely be awkward. While she volleyed this back and forth in her mind, Lon waited. His expression was a mixture of amusement and annoyance, the pen poised over the legal pad.

"Those poems you keep finding here. Don't you think it's a big coincidence that it's always you who finds them?" He didn't have to know she'd found a dozen or so others over the last few years. Lon was her only lead, and the poems had showed up in the shop more frequently ever since he started coming in for coffee a few times a week.

He took off his glasses. "I don't know, is it?"

She searched his face for some sign of recognition. Either Lon was a terrific actor or she was about to make a fool of herself.

"Are you Silas Penn?"

"Who?"

"Silas Penn. The writer of the poems."

When Lon snickered, Debi's face burned. She'd asked for it though.

"I'm sorry, but the idea of me writing poetry is pretty funny." He sat back in his chair.

"I had to ask."

"So that means you think I've been writing you...love poems?"

She was reluctant to answer. "Well, not anymore, judging by your reaction."

"I'm flattered."

"Wonderful, but I'm embarrassed."

"Don't be. I wish I was Silas Penn. Whomever he is, I'm jealous."

"Oh?"

"Writing poetry for a lady is so much more potent than any pick-up line."

"Well, I'm not sure either works for me."

Lon's eyebrows shot up. He nodded slowly, like he had her all figured out. "So you're one of those types?"

Silas Penn or not, this guy is a piece of work. She jammed her hand on her hip. "What type is that exactly?"

"The all-business, no-fun type."

Debi scratched behind her ear, debating on whether to check her reply or let Lon have it. She decided he wasn't worth the spike in her blood pressure if she engaged him. She had to finish cleaning the cases anyway.

"Even if I was the 'fun type' as you say, it's not doing him much good if he stays anonymous." She said this over her shoulder, determined not to give him one more minute of attention.

Lon tapped his pen on the table. "That's his problem. If it were me, I'd come right out and ask."

Debi stopped. "Ask what?" She wasn't doing a very good job at not engaging him.

"For a date."

She came back to him again and his eyes widened like he expected a sign, a go-ahead. She'd give him a sign, all right.

Debi pulled the rag from the crook of her arm, twirling it ominously close to his face.

"Too busy for dates." She stopped twirling. "Tell me this: Have you heard anyone at work say I'm selling my property?"

His expression changed. There was a pause. Then, "I can't talk about the company's business with a non-employee."

Debi laughed. "My property is *not* company business."

Lon put his pen away and slipped the pad into his leather case. "No, it's not."

"And here's another question: Does what I said at the Mesabi dinner have anything to do with most of the mine's employees not coming in here these last two weeks?"

He looked around as if the empty seats would answer for him. "I don't have any idea. I'm here, aren't I?" His smarmy grin told Debi he wasn't taking her seriously.

Lon Holder was the last guy she'd pick to be her mystery poet.

Chapter Eighteen

✿

Matt Stetman was the most talkative person Mick knew in Hendricks. He didn't usually mind Matt's endless banter, but today was different. Mick woke up on the right side of the bed that morning, but it was the side that preferred a quiet, reverent sort of day. Debi had been in his dreams throughout the night. Images of her face, the forest, and people on the periphery of their lives floated in and out of his subconscious, not making any sense. Still, the dreams left him feeling buoyant and contemplative. He needed quiet but Matt was the wrong person for that.

"One more section to go, and I think we can call it quits," Matt said, hoisting the end of one rail into the uppermost hole in the post. "I'm ready for a beer. How 'bout you?"

"I haven't earned it yet. Still have a couple more hours at the office." Mick tapped the top of the post a few more times with the mallet head then checked the level when he set it on the rail. Perfect.

"I'll tell you what, you earn it every day out here when it gets busy. I've seen what it takes to keep this place up. Worked here a summer myself when I got out of high school. Actually, it wasn't for the state park, it was for the waste management company contracted to—"

Matt's voice drifted away as Mick's thoughts returned to Debi. He hadn't heard from her in a few days. He'd called her twice each of the last two days, and they'd played phone tag the first day, then yesterday—nothing. She'd seemed distracted, distant when he visited the bakery too. And it wasn't because she was busy; the bakery was as empty as he'd ever seen it at eight o'clock in the morning. But she hadn't cancelled their trip to the Twin Cities today, so Mick was thankful for that. They'd have the four-hour drive to talk about whatever might be bothering her.

"Mick?"

Mick's gaze returned to Matt. "Sorry. I guess a bad night's sleep is finally catching up with me."

"Not a problem. Here, let's get this rail in," he said, holding on to one end while he waited for Mick. "As I was saying, it's getting busy out here. I wonder how visitor numbers will be affected when the mine grows. All that noise and dust won't make it easy to enjoy the great outdoors."

"I'm not certain the mine *will* grow. They're setting their sights on building on land that doesn't belong to them. I'm pretty sure the property owner isn't interested in selling."

Matt gave him a sidelong glance. "You're talking about

Debi Thomas, aren't you? Hey, you two have something going on? That's great. Someone mentioned you two might have hit it off."

That's what Mick disliked about living in a small town the most—rumors. "Yes, it's Debi's land I'm talking about. And as to your second question, I'm pretty sure we do. At least I'd like to think there's something happening." Mick wedged the other end of the rail into the post slot. He jammed it in with his gloved hand, gave it a couple taps with the mallet, then slid the level from his tool belt again.

Mick's expression must have registered his annoyance because Matt froze with the next rail in his arms. "Hey, it's not a big deal. No one was saying anything negative. It's just that, well, Debi Thomas is known for…keeping to herself."

"Yes, she is. And from what I know of her ex-husband, it's understandable."

"No kidding." Matt let out a long, low whistle. "Man, I tell you. Tom sure was a dog to her."

"Comparing him to a dog is an honor he doesn't deserve."

"True," Matt said, chuckling. "She let him stick around a lot longer than most people would. I couldn't stand to even sit next to him on a bar stool for an hour at Red's, let alone for the years he crashed at her place."

"Crashed? But they were married."

Matt made a face. "They were married for maybe a few years. After that it was only a marriage on paper from what I collected through the grapevine."

Mick nodded. "Yeah, I heard he checked out."

"It's funny. For as friendly as she seems at her shop, she's actually quite the opposite when she's anywhere else."

"I think it just takes a while for her to feel comfortable around people when she's out of her comfort zone."

"Truthfully, I tried getting a little friendlier with her a few years ago." He rested his arms on one of the posts. "You know, we grew up together here. I think Debi was actually in my brother's class, so she's"—Matt looked upward, closing one eye, thinking—"early thirties? Anyway, she was always kind of quiet, really smart, and hung out with the theater and band kids."

Mick smiled. "I can see that."

"Then I moved to the Twin Cities for a few years after high school, but the big city draw wore off after a while. So when I came back, there she was. And she was like this total stranger. Funny, outgoing, *hot*." His eyes popped out at that. "But she was married to Tom by then. So I waited until she divorced him."

A jealous twinge sparked in his chest at Matt's choice of words. "And?"

"She told me she wasn't interested. Just those words."

"At least she didn't string you along."

Matt shrugged. "Like I said, she seems closed off."

"There's definitely some trust issues." He said this under his breath, but Matt heard anyway.

"But good for you." Matt clapped him on the back. "If anyone deserves a little happiness in matters of the heart, it's you two. Debi's a real peach of a person."

Smiling, Mick hammered the next rail in place. "I think so too."

. . .

A HALF HOUR LATER, MICK LOADED THE LAST OF the supplies into the back of the ATV with Matt's help and said goodbye. He followed the River's Edge loop, a mowed trail that wove through a mile of the old growth forest, crossed the wide plank bridge over the Yarrow River, until it intersected with a dirt road. From there, it was a shortcut to the park office, though he regretted taking it after a minute of bouncing with all the loose tools clanking behind him. Ruts carved the road into a washboard, a result from the hard winter.

Mick slowed the ATV to a stop on the side of the road to secure the tools. After turning off the engine, he listened to the hush that fell over the forest. It was deafening. He was in the southernmost part of the park, near Sheevy's Lake, where the trees grew closer together once you wandered off the road. Cedar flags littered the ground and lichen-covered rocks poked out from beneath low shrubs. He'd finish his rounds of the reserved sites then head back to the office. Although it was still too early in the year for the park to be at full capacity, there was a surprising number of people camping for May.

As he sat there with the chill spring air ruffling his hair, he glanced toward the deer trail, off to his left, which ran for 200 yards through the trees. Then it turned abruptly to jog north alongside the temporary fence that marked the edge of the Lost Pine Mine prospect. He picked up the sound of the rumbling trucks running over the rough road near the mine's office. The guttural engines faded as they moved farther away.

A light rain had started. He pulled the hood over his head and took a deep breath to clear his lungs with the sweet spring air. It would be a shame if Gretchen's greed caused Debi's part of the woods to suffer. Truthfully, he didn't like to see large swaths of the forests swallowed up by industry, but his personal views didn't matter much. What Gretchen or Debi did with the land was none of his business. Mick was in the business of conservation, but there was plenty of industry using the land for its resources with their rightful deeds. Besides, his jurisdiction ended on the west side of High Road. Gretchen's prospect was on the other side of the road. No, he wouldn't try convincing Gretchen it was a mistake. That would cause even more friction. Yet he wasn't sure Debi could fight this battle on her own.

It picked at his conscience over the last few weeks, ever since he and Debi had become close. As much as he wanted to keep his convictions to himself, they became more intertwined with Debi's as the days wore on. Sooner or later, he'd have to choose—speak up in favor of developing the Lost Pine Mine prospect or support Debi's desire to preserve her land. And his preference had better lean toward the latter if Debi mattered to him.

As he sat on the ATV, feeling the mist dampen his face, it dawned on him. He'd already made his choice. How could he even pretend he hadn't? For years, he'd grieved Raila's death until time gave him the inevitable peace of mind. Stella was the reason. His work too. He had other priorities, and they helped him move on. But something was missing from his life—companionship. He was lonely. When it came down to it, though, he didn't know how to start a new relationship. So he'd only halfheartedly considered doing something about it.

Then Debi got him thinking about dating again. Her shop was Hendricks's gathering place. It was simple to see why. She was the type who brought people together. He liked to watch her at work, moving from table to table, refilling coffee, joking with the clientele in that easy banter of hers. She had a knack for making a shop full of people feel as if each one was her most favorite customer. For that reason, Mick found it took little effort to talk with her. And little by little, he looked forward to coming in a few times a week, and not only for his donut and coffee.

That was until he and Stella picked Debi up on the side of the road so many weeks ago. The dynamics of their relationship changed that afternoon; he could feel it. Debi was far from just a pretty, effervescent donut shop owner who made the best chocolate-raspberry bismarcks he'd ever tasted. She'd become more real to him—a divorcee who liked tending her gardens, reading crime novels by obscure British authors, and who valued her family roots. He liked how he felt when she was near. She made him feel whole again. How could he expect their relationship to deepen if he didn't help her?

His phone beeped in rapid succession, surprising him. A cell signal this far from the office was rare, which was why he usually left his phone on his desk, relying instead on a walkie-talkie. Mick patted his outer jacket pockets and then those of his zippered sweatshirt underneath it. There it was. He must have stuck the phone in there when he left the house and forgotten it was on him.

The first voicemail was from Gretchen. "Mick, I'm picking up Stella today. I hope you don't mind." He looked at the time on the message. It was sent two hours ago. Now it was well past lunch. Gretchen had let him know like he'd asked, but it was way after the fact. He shook his head. Once again Gretchen had the upper hand.

The other message was from school. *Uh-oh.* It was Stella's teacher, Angie. She'd try to reach him at the office phone, she said. The message was short, to the point. Mick played it again, trying to read the tone of her voice. Whatever it was, she didn't leave any hints.

He fired up the ATV again. It was time to get back anyway. Debi was due to meet him at the office in twenty minutes for their trip to the Twin Cities. He'd make a quick call to the school to see if this call from Angie Reil was something he could address on Monday.

Chapter Nineteen

D ebi wiped her hands on the apron after she'd plucked two donuts from the case and set them in the paper bag. She handed the bag to the woman with the little boy who'd been pulling at his mother's raincoat since they'd come inside the shop. No sooner was the bag in her hands than the little rascal snagged it, found a seat, and claimed one of the donuts as his own.

"I think I'm finally out of here," Debi said to Holly while checking the time on her phone. She should be on her way up Hill Road by now, but a rush of customers kept her from escaping fifteen minutes ago.

"It's about time. We'll be fine," Holly whispered when the woman left the counter. "You're off to a not-so-successful start to your new schedule."

"You're right. I'll get better as time goes by."

Debi decided a few days ago that Saturday mornings

after ten o'clock were now all hers. It was part of her live-life-to-the-fullest plan, to enjoy time outside the shop a little more—with someone besides herself. Debi could thank Mick for that. She'd never before had a reason to leave the shop to her two employees on the weekend. Debi slipped the apron over her head and hung it on the hook near the back door. Holly and her other part-timer Ronnie Hull would close by two.

Once she got home she'd change into walking shoes, then she and Harley would run a couple loops around the woods, on the trails her grandfather cleared of timber and underbrush so many decades ago. Her usual weekends consisted of time spent alone—reading, crocheting, working on home projects, walking with Harley—until she had to be back to the shop in the wee hours of Tuesday morning. She wasn't used to rushing around on a Saturday morning after she left work, but she and Mick had plans. Big plans. An overnight trip to the Twin Cities. They'd visit the gourmet pastry shop in St. Paul she'd heard opened last month. And she was really looking forward to the mystery dinner theater, which was Mick's idea. She'd never been to one. Her aunt Carrie, an innkeeper in the Presbitt Historic neighborhood, would host them for the night, too, something she'd been begging Debi to take her up on for years.

Debi's cheeks burned thinking about spending practically a whole weekend with Mick, and she silently cursed herself. What was all this blushing about lately? She never figured herself the type for this nonsense, though to be fair to herself, there hadn't been a man worthy enough to blush over in a long time.

TWO HOURS LATER, AFTER SHE'D DROPPED HARLEY off at the boarder, Debi pulled into the state park lot next to Mick's truck, and walked into the park office. She'd wait for him while he wrapped up a few things inside.

Mick stood at the counter in the welcome area, studying a large map. He looked up and grinned.

"Hey there," she said. "I know I'm a few minutes early, but I ran out of things to do. A little anxious, I guess."

Mick rolled up the map. He'd already changed from his park uniform into jeans and a thin fleece pullover. Debi made a mental note to remember how good he looked in it, the material stretching across his shoulders, when his birthday rolled around next month. Debi wouldn't mind seeing him wear a few more.

He came from around the counter. "I know. Me too." Mick snapped his fingers. "I keep meaning to tell you: I think I found your guy who was skulking around the woods by your place."

"Seriously? Who?"

"Justine and I were in here the other day when a guy showed up, asking about morel mushrooms. Said he was from the Minnesota Morel Society."

"I didn't know there was such a thing."

Mick shrugged. "Neither did I. We occasionally have people hunting them in the park, but they're not supposed to take them. I guess he was trying to get around the park rules by going over to your side of the road."

"Except he was trespassing on my land. It's about a month too early for morels anyway. I wish he would have talked to me instead of hiding."

"That's what I told him."

"Well, that's a relief. I can deal with mushroom hunters better than I can creepy lurkers."

Debi shrugged off her jacket, tossing it over her arm. She walked into his outstretched arms, and they stood that way in the quiet, empty office for a few moments, Debi basking in the breathtaking sensation of being held again after all these years.

"This probably isn't part of your job description, is it?" Her voice was muffled as she pressed her face against his shoulder, the heady scent of soap and pinesap filling her senses.

Mick hugged her tighter. "Not really, but I can try getting it changed."

Debi looked up into his face and smiled. His dark eyes held her captive.

"But then it's not a very productive use of my time here," he whispered.

The throaty purr in his voice sent goosebumps rippling up her back. Reluctantly, Debi pulled away. "I guess we'll have time for this later." She tucked hair behind her ears. "My aunt is looking forward to meeting you, by the way. She's been dying to get me to stay at her inn."

He stepped back. "You're sure it's not an intrusion? I feel guilty taking her up on a free night."

"Not at all. If she found out we paid for a room in town without thinking of her first, she'd be miffed. Where's Stella spending the night?"

"With her friend Brit." Mick walked around the counter again, straightening paper piles and checking his cell phone. "Speaking of Stella, I'm waiting for a phone call, then we can head out."

As if on cue, Mick's cell phone rang. He fished it out of his back pocket and glanced at the screen. "Gotta take this in the back room," he said with an apologetic look. "Hopefully it won't be too long."

"No worries. Take your time. The Twin Cities aren't going anywhere."

She watched him as he walked down the hall. His muffled voice soon faded as he moved farther into one of the boardrooms and closed the door. Debi walked around the office, studying the maps on the walls. She glanced at a brochure for canoeing the Boundary Waters and another for Voyagers National Park until the picture frames on his desk caught her eye. Debi put the brochures back in their holders and walked over to Mick's desk.

Most of the photos were of Stella. School photos. Her wearing a softball uniform and balancing a bat on her shoulder. As a baby, sitting in Raila's lap. Debi picked up the mother-and-daughter photo. She studied Raila's light features and the unmistakable eyes linking her to Stella. A pang rippled in her stomach. This was his wife. Was she the love of his life? Debi wondered if she could ever fill that hole. She wasn't even sure she could fill it for anyone. She was divorced. Closed off and too focused on herself, Debi's mom liked to tell her when the inevitable questions about her love life—or lack of—came up in conversation. Debi set the photo down.

The office was quiet except for the hum of Mick's distant voice. They were the only ones inside the park office. The other two rangers on duty must have been on their lunch break or patrolling the park. Debi sat down to wait in the swivel chair. When she did, the chair tilted too far backward and she bumped the console behind her, causing a chain-reaction mini disaster. A water bottle, pencil holder, and empty Tupperware container scattered across the floor. She hit the computer keyboard with her forearm as she bent down to collect everything, and the monitor lit up.

She set the things back on the desktop, careful not to upset anything else. When her eyes fell on the monitor, she paused. Debi would have ignored the email on the computer screen if her address hadn't jumped out at her immediately: E2254 High Road.

Debi scooted the chair closer.

It was an email from Gretchen Hinsdorff to Mick:

"…be sure to include these details in the report to Consolidated Iron. The high quality of the new addition of Ms. Thomas's property needs to be emphasized as this is precisely why they are considering the purchase of the Lost Pine Mine prospect through Mesabi Holdings…"

Ms. Thomas? They were talking about her and her land as if she didn't own it.

"…Time is of the essence, Mick. If you'll get back to me as soon as

you can, I'd like to get this moving in a timely fashion before they
change their minds…"

Worse than that, it sounded like Mick was helping Gretchen acquire it.

Debi slumped back into the chair. The room spun.

How could I have been so blind?

Of course Mick had a vested interest in Gretchen's company. They were still family, bound by Raila and Stella. All of Mick's talk about his squabbles with Gretchen had only been partially true. In the end, they were both out to help grow Gretchen's company for Stella's sake. And Mick's goodwill gesture on the day she'd been at her mailbox was the perfect opportunity to get close to her.

The pounding in her ears was deafening by the time she finished reading the letter. Debi had to get out of there before Mick finished the call. She couldn't face him, not after reading this. Not after learning he'd been working with Gretchen behind her back the whole time. Her gut feeling had been right. She couldn't count on anyone but herself. How foolish she was to believe it might be different this time with Mick. *Trust me,* he'd said. Debi knew better, but she had let her guard down. All for some silly, happily-ever-after fantasy.

She grabbed her coat and hurried to the door, hearing Mick whistling as his footsteps echoed in the hall.

"Sorry, that took so—" she heard him say before she closed the door behind her.

Don't look back.

The wind howled through the parking lot, whipping the

hair around her face. Everything seemed to be in motion—the trees, the birds, her whole world. She reached for her car door, wanting to slow down the spinning.

Don't look back.

"Debi—wait!" Mick called, his voice almost lost in the howling wind.

She pretended to not hear him. It was best this way.

Chapter Twenty

✥

Mick stood in the foyer of the park office, watching Debi wheel out of the parking space and drive away. He'd called to her several times as she hurried across the lot, the wind whipping her hair like wildfire, but she hadn't even looked at him.

He'd gone back inside to get his phone and keys, puzzled as to why she was mad enough to leave without an explanation, to ditch their plans for their overnight trip to the Twin Cities. Then he saw the email on his monitor when he grabbed his keys off the desk. Of course she'd stormed off. He wouldn't blame her if she never wanted to speak to him again. But then, she only knew half the story.

As much as he wanted to chase after Debi, it would have to wait. Stella was his priority. He'd finally talked to Stella's teacher, who relayed the message from Gretchen: Stella didn't want to return to school after lunch. She was upset about something. So Gretchen had dropped her off at home.

Luckily, Mick's house was a five-minute drive from the park office. In that short time, the ball of worry ballooned into a problem he'd never had before—the feeling things had spun out of control. Mick pulled into his drive and hurried inside the house. In the family room, his daughter was sunk into the overstuffed armchair near the wood stove, flipping absentmindedly through a book. She looked up when he walked into the room and frowned.

Stella's face was blotchy and drawn. Fierce tears rather than the self-pitying kind flowed when Stella was hurt. The downward slashes of her eyebrows were proof. Normally, he'd leave her alone, let her decompress in her own bubble of misery, but there were too many questions needing answers. She glowered at him like a feral cat as he came toward her. Mick sat on the ottoman in front of her.

"Let's talk." Mick nudged her knee with his fist.

"I'd rather not."

He'd have to navigate this minefield carefully.

"Did something happen at school?"

"Nope."

"Did something happen at lunch?"

She tossed the book onto the floor. It hit with a hollow thud. "I said I don't want to talk about it."

"So that means something happened with your grandmother. I got the message from her that you two were going to lunch after the fact."

Another murderous look.

Mick rolled his neck, feeling the tension crouching in his shoulders. What he wouldn't do for one of Debi's shoulder massages right now. Her hands had worked pure magic the other day, kneading the knots from his muscles after work. No chance of that happening anytime soon, though.

"Stella. I can't help you if you won't talk to me."

"Grandma called me selfish."

"She *what?*"

She threw a hand up. "I know, right? She said I wasn't thinking of her and all she's done for me."

Mick couldn't wrap his head around Gretchen saying that to Stella. As awful as she could be, Gretchen fawned over Stella. Her granddaughter was her link to Raila after all. This was a new low.

He tried not to let the shock show. "I'm sorry. That must have been pretty hurtful coming from her," he said in a low voice.

Stella swiped angrily at the tears on her cheeks. "She also wanted me to talk about Debi. To find out what Debi was planning to do with the property."

"What did she say exactly?"

"She wanted to know if I've heard you and Debi talk about the prospect. Grandma said she needs to buy it or the company won't make it long enough for me to take it over." Stella narrowed her eyes. "But that's not true at all. All of her other prospects make plenty of money."

Mick reached for her hand, but Stella drew away and crossed her arms. Her expression grew even more fierce.

"But I told her I didn't want to say any more. I like Debi. I don't want to help Grandma."

Mick nodded. "You did the right thing. I'm sure it was hard though, standing up to her."

"Actually, it wasn't hard at the time. She made me so

mad it was pretty easy to tell her how I felt. I don't like feeling used." Stella picked at a stray thread on her sleeve.

"I understand how you feel. I don't like when people use me either."

"Did Grandma use you too?"

He almost mentioned Gretchen's visit to the park office. But Stella had enough of a burden dealing with her own betrayal. No need to involve her in adult problems.

"No," he said. *She tried.*

"So what are you going to do?"

"I'm not sure. This is really between them."

Stella looked up at him. "But don't you like Debi?"

"Of course I do."

"Then why wouldn't you help her? Why would you let Grandma try to bully her?"

Mick leaned back, thinking. He'd gone back and forth in his mind about this very question. Why should he get involved if Debi hadn't asked him for help? But Stella was right. If he cared about Debi, he could at least offer advice, be a sounding board. And if she wanted to keep her business private, then he'd back off.

"That's a good question. It's not that simple." Mick stood up and ran his fingers through his hair. "I'd better call the school and let them know you're home."

"Dad?"

Mick stopped. "Yes?"

"Do you want to know what made Grandma the maddest?"

"What?"

"She said she thinks of me in every business decision she

makes, but I told her I didn't care. If she hurts people, I don't want anything to do with that company."

Mick looked down at his shoes to hide the smile. "I'm sure that made her day."

"I think I want to be a nurse anyway."

He chuckled, and leaning down, kissed the top of her head.

"You'll make a fantastic nurse or whatever you choose to do."

AFTER DINNER, MICK TOOK HIS PHONE OUTSIDE and sat on the front steps. He punched in Debi's number again, steeling himself against whatever anger she threw his way. He owed her an explanation. Hopefully, she'd let him talk long enough for him to give her one. It rang, his heart sinking with each unanswered ring, and he was about to hang up to avoid getting her voicemail for the sixth time, when the call connected.

"Since you can't take the hint that unanswered voicemails mean I don't want to talk, I thought I'd just come out and say it: I don't want to talk," she said in a clipped tone. If they were face to face, Mick was sure she'd be speaking through her teeth.

"Wait. Don't hang up. I—"

"I mean it, Mick. And just so you know, I wasn't snooping. I accidentally hit your keyboard and the message popped up."

"That's not what I thought at all. Besides, that's not the issue."

"It most certainly IS the issue. Gretchen's email proves you were working together all along."

"I know it looks like that—"

"I'm serious. You have nothing to say I want to hear right now. Goodbye, Mick."

He stared at his phone long after her voice cut off, wondering how he could extricate himself from this mess. Mick shook his head and stuffed the phone back into his pocket. What did Stella tell Gretchen, that she didn't want to be involved with the company if it meant Gretchen had to hurt people?

How had his twelve-year-old daughter learned to pick a side and he hadn't?

Chapter Twenty-One

The weekend passed with no more calls from Mick. Debi took advantage of the quiet to finish laying the mosaic walkway from her shed to the garden gate, finding the intricate work of arranging colored tiles and chipped pieces of china in wet cement therapeutic. If someone chose to lurk in her woods again, she didn't care. If someone left tire tracks through her property, she didn't care. Her intention to wallow in self-pity for a few days would not be interrupted. Debi's head throbbed from spinning with so many questions, but her heart hurt more.

Tuesday morning brought the usual quiet to the shop and Debi's mood darkened. Red and Tonti Hill came by in the first hour, and so did Donna Marconi, but then business died.

"You forgot to turn on the 'open' sign. Maybe that's why no one is here," Holly said, pointing.

Sure enough, the neon light was dark. That *had* to be it.

Debi flipped the switch on near the window and immediately spotted Gretchen heading from her car across the street to the shop. Outside, the wind was fierce, whipping the woman's black coat around her legs like bat wings. Debi steeled herself as if she were the one fighting the elements, but it was only for the confrontation to come. Gretchen never came to the shop alone. Something was in the air, and it wasn't just the scent of scones baking in the oven.

If Gretchen weren't such an insufferable person, she might be an attractive woman. She had the kind of presence that made people take notice when she entered a room. Tall without being oafish and trim, the older woman moved like someone half her age, but that dictatorial personality she was known for overshadowed her good looks. Unfortunately, Gretchen gave more attention to building her company than the people who helped her along that journey. She could be as well respected as anyone in Hendricks if she were half as selfish. And she relished conflict. Debi experienced it firsthand.

The door swung open with brutal force, pulling Gretchen inside, depositing her on the welcome mat. Her poise momentarily disrupted, Gretchen brushed herself off and looked around with feigned concern.

"Where is everyone today?"

"Good morning, Gretchen." Debi went behind the counter. She needed the physical barrier between them. "You missed the rush."

The older woman's expression was skeptical. "I had hoped the rumors I heard weren't true."

Debi sighed. *Here we go.* "What rumors?"

"That business was down. That you were thinking of closing."

She stared at Gretchen. "I have never once thought of closing, and no, business is going quite nicely, thank you. What do you need?"

Gretchen's smile was thin. "I'm happy to hear that." She motioned toward a table. "Can we sit down for a minute?"

If she'd had even one customer, Debi would have used the excuse of being busy. But her empty shop betrayed her. Resigned, she showed Gretchen to the nearest table.

Gretchen reached into the leather tote on her lap and pulled out a white envelope. She set it on the table.

"We haven't had a real conversation in a while," Gretchen said.

"There's nothing for us—"

Gretchen put her hand up. "Let me finish please. I'm aware there's talk around town—rumors, if you will—and I don't much like the speculation. Facts make things happen. So I'd like to clear the air and maybe make something happen." Gretchen looked at her directly. "I think we both know what the other wants. But we're too afraid the other is going to get in our way."

Debi coughed. "I'm afraid?"

"I only meant it as a euphemism. Of course you're not afraid. You're a businesswoman. A risk-taker."

Mick warned her Gretchen was a master manipulator.

That was a compliment she would graciously accept from most everyone else. Coming from Gretchen, it put her on the defensive. The words didn't ring true coming from their source.

"What exactly do you want from me?"

Gretchen gave her a level gaze. "Your property."

"You can't have it." Debi paused, waiting for Gretchen's reaction, but the older woman sat silently, lips pressed together. "And what do you think I want from you?"

"You'd like me to go away."

A short, humorless laugh escaped Debi. "That's pretty much it."

Gretchen nodded and leaned forward. "Listen, I understand your reservations. It's your home. Your family has been a part of this community for a long time. They helped build it, for Pete's sake."

"Then how can you even ask me to sell?"

Gretchen folded her hands together on top of the envelope. She looked down at them clasped together, weighing her answer.

"Because family is important to me too. My husband and I built Mesabi Holdings from nothing. Then when he passed, I kept it going. I made it better. The Lost Pine Mine prospect would be the crowning jewel on top of the other prospects I own." Gretchen paused when her voice cracked on the last word. She rubbed her hands together. "The company would have been my legacy to my daughter. Now that she's gone, I want to keep it strong for Stella, my granddaughter."

"I know Stella."

Gretchen glanced up. For a split second, her eyes rrowed. Then she gave Debi a small smile. "Yes, of course ιu do."

Debi sat back against the chair. As long as they were ɔeing honest, Debi couldn't hold it in. "I saw the email. I know you and Mick are working together."

"What email?"

"I don't blame him for helping you with the reports. You are family, after all. It opened my eyes at the right time, before I—"

Gretchen leaned forward. "When did you see this email?"

"What does it matter? But answer this: What makes you think I'd hand over my property just to make you a richer woman?"

Gretchen pushed the envelope toward her. "Open it."

Debi slid her finger under the flap, all the while keeping her eyes locked on Gretchen's. She slipped the paper out of the envelope.

A check. A very *large* check.

Debi blinked at the numbers. She made sure the figure matched its written form on the line underneath her name in case it was a mistake.

But there was no mistake.

One and a half million dollars.

Debi swallowed hard.

"This is a joke. My property is worth maybe a third of that."

"I understand you're shocked. I would be too. What I'm

offering is way above fair market value. But it also shows I respect your sacrifice."

Debi hated that she was near speechless.

Gretchen refolded her hands. "You could be a very rich woman too," she said, her voice almost a whisper.

Debi cleared her throat. "I can't make a decision today."

"I understand completely." Gretchen nodded to the check Debi still held in her slightly shaking hand. "I'm going to leave that here. Think about it."

Debi watched Gretchen get up to leave.

"What happens if I don't sell?"

Gretchen paused. Her expression tightened despite the thin smile. "Call me when you reach a decision."

Debi watched Gretchen leave. Only when she was across the street again, inside her car, did Debi look at the check again. She felt nauseous. The amount was more than she could fathom.

She slipped the check into the bottom of her bag and finished wiping down the last table. Then the sugar packets in the tiny wicker baskets on each table needed straightening. She stripped the flyers with expired dates from the bulletin board and swept behind the counter, though the floor was spotless.

Debi propped the broom against the wall and groaned.

One and a half million dollars.

Imagine the things she could do with the money. That European vacation she always wanted to take was a real possibility. She could hire another employee so she could cut back on her hours even more. One and a half million dollars opened up a lot of options, ones Debi never dreamed she'd be considering.

And what if she wanted to sell the bakery and move somewhere else, make a fresh start? Now that Mick and her...well, never mind about that. She'd look to the future, not dwell on the past.

Chapter Twenty-Two

Mick sat in his truck a block away, waiting for Gretchen to come out of Debi's shop. He'd almost parked behind Gretchen's Lexus a few minutes ago until he realized it was her car. Instead, he circled the block and parked at a distance. She didn't need to know he was here. He wouldn't put it past her to stage a scene if she thought Mick was out to compromise whatever she plotted against Debi.

Thirty minutes later, Mick shuffled the newspaper he'd been reading to pass the time and almost missed Gretchen before she got into her car. Was there an extra bounce in her step, or was that his imagination? He could sit there all day and guess what the subtleties in Gretchen's mannerisms meant, or he could get out of his hiding place and go talk to Debi himself. If he knew Gretchen, she'd made Debi an offer. It was none of his business, so he wouldn't dare ask, but he hoped Debi would talk to him at least. Already he was way more involved in the situation than he'd counted on.

Mick saw Debi through the front window, sweeping the floor. By the time he opened the door, she was seated again at one of the tables. Debi startled for a second, then went back to looking more relaxed than he'd expected. Her feet were on a chair, ankles crossed. A half-empty coffee mug sat in front of her.

"Hi there," she said softly.

Mick sat down across from her. "I saw Gretchen leave."

She raised her brows while tracing the rim of her mug with her index finger but stayed quiet.

He really wanted to talk about the email, to explain what she thought she'd read wasn't the truth at all. The words sat at the back of his throat. Mick's fear of saying the wrong thing, of snapping the thread of their fragile relationship at this point, was real. He felt guilty enough for having to explain his way out of what looked obvious on the surface. *Please let her listen and think about another possibility.*

"She made me an offer for my property," Debi said before he could speak. Her finger stopped and she looked at him. "Though you probably already know that."

"Debi, I—"

She shook her head abruptly. "Stop. Let me talk."

Two customers came in. Holly, her part-timer, appeared at the counter to help. Mick didn't miss the girl's wide-eyed expression when she spotted Debi and him together. So Debi must have shared something with Holly about him. Was it favorable, from before Debi read the email? Or did Holly hear he was in league with Gretchen?

Debi watched Holly wait on the customers for a few moments, like she was gathering her thoughts. Finally, she looked at him again. Her eyes were sad.

"I could take that trip to Europe I've always dreamed of. Move, start over. There's nothing to keep me here anyway." She looked away when Mick opened his mouth to protest, but she kept talking. "I have no family nearby most of the time. My parents come back here a few months out of the year. My brother and his family even less. I have no kids. My customers are the closest I have to relatives in Hendricks."

"You can't sell the shop. It's practically a Hendricks landmark."

Debi shrugged. "And it would still be a landmark when I sell it to someone else."

Mick ran his hands through his hair in frustration and sat back heavily in the chair. He didn't like her tone. So resigned and unemotional.

"Think about what you're saying. What about the generations who cleared that land, built your home? And the graves? That place isn't some random house sitting on a piece of land. It's your home. It molded you."

"I'll have the graves moved." Debi turned to look out the window as if something happening outside was more important than what was going on right in front of her. "The sky's the limit for me. I can do anything I want with the amount she offered me."

Mick pressed his hands together in front of him. "Debi, think about this. Gretchen has played both of us against each other. Don't you see? It's all about getting what she wants. About winning the game."

"I have a lot to think about, Mick. And I don't want to talk about it anymore with you until I sort it out in my own mind first."

Two more people came into the shop. Debi looked back at him then stood. "But I think it's too good of an offer to pass up. Now I have to get back to work."

Mick had to make her understand. "That email you read. It's not what you think."

Debi started toward the counter but stopped. "I'm not sure how I can interpret what I read any other way."

"Gretchen did ask for my help. That's true. What you didn't see was my response to her. I refused to help based on not wanting to get in between you two. Now I see it might've been a mistake."

"How so?"

"I should have taken a side—yours."

Debi looked at the ceiling and shook her head. "I can make my own decisions."

"I'm aware of that. But isn't it nice when someone has your back?"

She huffed. "Truthfully, I'm not sure. My limited experience with romantic relationships tells me no, it's not a guarantee of support."

The door chimed. Another customer came in. Time wasn't on his side here. She had to understand he wasn't working against her.

"I'm not sure what else I can say to convince you I'm innocent. I wouldn't hurt you like that. I'll say it again: You can trust me." He put his hands up when she balked. "No, I'm not *him*. I *mean* it."

"Like I said, I have a lot of thinking to do." Debi gave him a wary look. "Now I need to get back to work."

Debi waited behind the case for the next person in line to place an order. She refused to look at Mick. When it was clear Debi wouldn't get a break in business anytime soon, Mick headed for the door.

Outside, the wind had died down and a soft drizzle fell. The sun fought the clouds in its way, trying to break free and brighten the day, but it didn't look promising. Mick stood on the sidewalk for a minute, hands in his pockets, looking across the street toward the lake. A dull sun, fleeting between the dense bank of clouds, touched the water as if casting jewels across its surface at random intervals.

Mick walked toward his car, feeling like his heart was splitting in half with each step he took away from her.

Chapter Twenty-Three

※❀※

The next morning, Debi moved in robotlike fashion. She frosted two dozen rings but didn't remember preparing the glaze or sliding them into the case. She took an order from Darci for Blueberry Point Lodge but couldn't find the order slip ten minutes after she got off the phone. Tables were wiped down, garbage deposited in the dumpster, and dough prepared for the afternoon, but they were phantom tasks, finished by some nameless person in another dimension.

Debi stood on tiptoe at the bulletin board, pulling down more flyers advertising events that had already happened. She paused and pressed her fingers against her temples.

"I don't know what's wrong with me." *Liar*.

Behind the counter, Holly frowned. "Maybe you shouldn't drive if you don't feel well. I can ask my mom if she'll take you home."

Debi turned around and leaned against the wall.

"Thank you, but no. I'll be fine. It's only a little headache from not sleeping well."

Holly looked unsure but went back to piping the edges of sugar cookies.

The bulletin board was all but clear except for the handful of Silas Penn poems left behind. She studied the last one, the poem Lon Holder had brought her on the day she confronted him about being the mystery poet. Her faced burned at the memory. She hadn't embarrassed herself in such spectacular fashion in a long time. But she was thankful. It would have been disappointing if Lon had been Silas Penn. Maybe she'd never find out who had written them, a small disappointment. In a corner of her heart, Debi realized she'd fallen in love with the little gems. Or maybe her melancholy was spilling over into everything and she was being overly dramatic.

Debi straightened the stack of flyers, looked around the empty shop, and sighed.

"I think I'm going to take off a little sooner than I planned after all."

Holly stopped piping. "No problem. I'll finish these, then start on your list before closing. Shouldn't be any trouble," she said. "Go get some rest."

LATER THAT AFTERNOON, DEBI WOKE UP TO THE early evening sun casting stripes on her wall as it blazed through the blinds. She'd had a somewhat long, restless nap on the couch, and now she was stiff and fuzzy-headed. Her stomach grumbled in protest at missing dinner. Harley, too, looked especially irritated. His eyes darted between her and his bowl sitting empty on the kitchen floor.

Her dreams were filled with the thunder of falling trees, and rain, and fleeting shadows in the forest. Her mother materialized for a moment behind one of the trees but then she morphed into Debi's father, then her high school softball coach, then Lon Holder. Debi rarely dreamed.

She begrudgingly made herself a baked potato, feeling obligated to eat, but the first bite was tasteless, and she pushed it aside. Earlier, she'd found a blank sheet of paper and left it on the table. Now she stared at it next to her, wondering where to start. It taunted her.

After a few minutes, she divided the sheet in half, wrote "pro" on one side, "con" on the other. That was what reasonable people did, right? They made lists to weigh advantages against the bad stuff. The first positive came to mind right away: money. Yet when she finished the list later, a big, fat dollar sign was the only advantage listed on the left-hand side. At least a dozen negatives—no more baking, PACKING!, leaving Hendricks, the promise she'd made to herself that she'd preserve her family home—filled in the right-hand column. Debi could list even more.

But that dollar sign. She'd made it big on purpose. It was a *big* deal.

Debi blew the air out of her cheeks. She drummed her pen on the tabletop.

Tap, tap, tap.

That check was a cement block chained to her, weighing her down. What was she going to do? Gretchen counted on Debi taking the offer, but this was her home.

Mick's words flashed into her consciousness. *"It's your home. It molded you."*

Her bag sat on the chair beside her. She fished for the envelope and finding it, set it on the table. It had become an albatross, keeping her from thinking about anything else.

Tap, tap, tap.

Debi pulled out the check and stared at all those zeroes.

Those numbers wouldn't replace the house, the land, the woods and the little family plot. She'd lied to Mick. Debi had no intention of moving the headstones. They belonged right where they stood. Debi caught herself nodding slightly, and then she smiled. Of course.

THE NAP AND HER SCATTERED THOUGHTS KEPT Debi up throughout the night until first light peeked through the curtains in her bedroom. Her head still fuzzy, she sat up in bed, staring into the semi-darkness of her room. Harley jumped onto the bed and settled next to her, laying his head on her lap.

"What should we do?" She stroked Harley's back as the dog lifted his head and whined. She could see him cocking his head at her.

"I know. It's a hard decision."

As if he understood, Harley stretched his body against the full length of hers and moaned in all his doggy misery.

Debi chuckled. "Thanks for the insight. I knew I could count on you."

She lay there, playing the conversation she'd had with

Mick in the bakery. He'd looked so hurt, so desperate to get her to listen. Something he said echoed in her mind:

I should have taken your side.

Was it too late?

No, it wasn't. It couldn't be. Mick was there for her then, and he hadn't changed his mind. His loyalty wasn't frivolous. She'd have to learn that trust wasn't synonymous with losing her self-worth. Mick wasn't Tom, could *never* be him. Debi had to trust herself again too.

Debi grabbed her jacket off the hook near the door and was in her car within seconds. She didn't care that it was six in the morning. She didn't care if Mick didn't want to speak to her after she cut him off the other day. Debi wanted him to know she'd made a decision, that he'd helped her understand. And she needed to see him.

When Debi pulled up to the house, the craziness of the early morning visit registered. She was still in her pajamas. She'd forgot to comb her hair. Now that she was here, Debi didn't quite know how she'd wake Mick without disturbing Stella too. Maybe she should go back home, wait for a more reasonable hour, and call instead.

As she weighed her options, Mick opened the front door.

Barefoot, coffee mug in hand, he came down the steps toward her car, a worried frown on his face. His faded, oversized sweatshirt and the plaid flannel pants were a delicious distraction. Debi could hardly keep her eyes on his face.

"Sorry, I didn't mean to come this early." She winced. It was a silly thing to say. Of course she meant to come.

"Is something wrong?" He gave her a once-over.

"I'm not going to sell."

He took a sip of his coffee in an unhurried way, keeping his focus on her, probably wondering if her wishy-washiness was confined to the moment or a long-term affliction.

"Why?"

She pulled her sweatshirt close around her neck when a chill crept down the front of her shirt. "Can we go inside?"

Mick lifted his arm toward the porch and followed her in without another word.

The house was still dark, save for the light over the kitchen sink. Mick switched on the dimmer so a soft golden glow lit the room.

"Want coffee?"

Debi nodded. "Please."

"I'm toasting a bagel. I can make you one."

"That'd be great."

They walked into the kitchen where Mick took another mug from the cabinet and filled it. She waited while he stirred in a teaspoon of creamer and a little cube of sugar—he kept a bowl of sugar cubes on hand now—just how she liked it. He glanced at her as he handed over the mug. His eyes were hooded and a little bloodshot. Debi wondered if she'd given him a restless night.

"So..."

He leaned against the counter. "So?"

Debi breathed deeply. "I was almost seduced by Gretchen's offer, but in the end, I decided I can't let it go."

"What changed your mind?"

"The connection between the land and my family is too

strong." She held the mug in one hand, swirled the spoon with the other. "You were right."

"I'm happy for you," he said in a flat tone.

As he waited for the toaster, Debi tried reading his expression. She'd wait until they sat down before offering more of an explanation and an apology. She owed him one after comparing him to Tom at least.

While Mick worked in the kitchen, Debi studied the elegant family tree on his wall again. She liked that they had an appreciation for their ancestral roots in common. The crinkled parchment paper background looked old, but someone had made it so. It was a beautiful piece of art, a pen-and-ink sketch of a sprawling tree. Silhouettes of people in vintage clothing filled in the empty spaces among the names and dates written in flowing, gilded script.

She stepped closer to the framed print. Her eyes were drawn to the top, where Stella and Mick sat on the tips of the uppermost branches along with Mick's sister's family. Below them, their parents and grandparents. She lingered over the names and dates, enjoying the musical quality of the old-fashioned names as she heard them in her mind's ear, as the generations of Mick's family wound backward in time.

William and Sally (Eldrich) Graham, grandparents.

Michael and Elizabeth (Blanchard) Henderson, grandparents.

Eldrid Geoffrey Henderson, great-grandfather, and Lilith (See) Henderson, great-grandmother.

Walter Silas Henderson, great-great-grandfather, Hilda Penelope (Alamati) Henderson, great-great-grandmother.

Alistair Fraser—

Something made her pause. She lingered on the last name.

Alistair Fraser.

No, that wasn't it. Something had stopped her from reading further, but what?

Debi scanned the top half of the tree again, reading the names aloud under her breath. She almost made it to the end where she'd stopped before, but the names of his great-great-grandparents caught her eye.

She swallowed.

Walter Silas Henderson, great-great-grandfather.

Hilda Penelope (Alamati) Henderson, great-great-grandmother.

She stared at the names. *Walter Silas. Hilda Penelope.*

Was it a coincidence, these names? Her mind raced, trying to piece together similarities.

No, it couldn't be. Yet, here were these names popping out at her.

Silas and Penelope.

He was a regular at the shop, so the random appearance of poems wouldn't be impossible. And reading the Burns selection at his ancestry presentation showed he appreciated poetry. It was so crazy to think about that she laughed out loud.

Was Mick...Silas Penn?

Blood rushed in her ears. She pressed a hand to her chest, trying to calm the thudding beneath her fingers, and took a step back.

Feet shuffled on the floor behind her. When she turned

around, Mick held the plate with her bagel. His eyes were luminous.

"Mick, what—?"

He was quiet, watchful.

She pointed to the frame as if she needed proof for the questions racing through her mind. "You're…Silas Penn?"

Silence. Then a slight nod.

"The same one who—who…the poems in the newspaper?"

"The one and only." He set the plate on the counter.

"But this—this has been going on for years. And at work? Why do you leave poems there of all places?"

He stuck his hands in his pockets and stared at the floor.

Debi stepped closer. "Why there?"

When he looked up at her, she knew the answer. His expression was soft, pleading, anxious.

"Because you inspire me. You have for a long time," he said, a little whisper of a smile lighting his face.

She tried to remember how long she'd been finding poems there, but the realization of this news clouded any rational thought. They were funny, awkward, heartfelt, and she'd loved every single one. Now here was this man, admitting to her he'd been writing them for years. *For her.*

She took another step forward, close enough that Mick reached out for her hand. Debi melted against him, the ocean sound in her ears now silenced by the sensation of his breath in her hair.

"I'm shocked."

He huffed into her hair. "I'm relieved."

"I don't know what to say."

"I do."

Debi drew back. His expression, tired and drawn, was also full of emotion.

"I love you," he said.

She studied his face for a sign he might not be serious. Debi let out a little laugh. Maybe it mixed with a sob, she didn't know, but happiness, surprise, and fear overwhelmed her all at once. Debi almost said it too, but the words caught in her throat. When she gripped the counter to steady herself, Mick reached for her again. They stood that way for a long time, soothed by the silence of the morning, and finally—*finally*—having found what had long been missing.

Chapter Twenty-Four

The canoe scraped along the lake's rocky bottom as Mick pushed it away from shore. He hopped in, rocking it wildly from side to side before Debi gripped the sides, trying to steady the swaying boat. They took up the paddles to ease their way farther into the lake, toward Lone Tree Islet, a few hundreds yards away. The islet was a pile of basalt rocks, big and small, and twenty yards across with a cluster of scrub brush and one lone cedar tree standing at its center. The tree grew crooked, wind-whipped from decades of being battered by the elements. A little length of beach, rocky but quaint, beckoned. Mick had come out here only once with Stella a few years ago for a picnic lunch and a little fishing.

He squinted toward the east. "How much time do we have before I need to get you back for your book club?"

Over Debi's shoulder, the early morning sun was a dull orange orb on the horizon. A light breeze ruffled the hair around her face. When she turned to look behind her, the sun broke through the thin bank of clouds, its light streaking toward them so it crowned her head with a halo. Mick marveled at the resplendent moment, thinking he'd have to write about it soon. He'd never written a poem about hair. He wondered if Debi would think it strange. So far, she hadn't said that any of his poems crossed the line. Still, an entire poem devoted to her hair might be over the top.

"An hour and a half, maybe." Debi's brows dipped, a small smile curling her lips. "What are you smiling about?"

"Something possibly a little weird."

Her eyes widened. "Intriguing. Do tell."

"An idea for a poem. About you."

"Now I really want to know. Especially if it's a strange poem about me."

"It might be too strange at this point."

"That doesn't scare me. I like strange things."

Mick chuckled. She did indeed. He found Debi had a passion for some unusual collections. She liked foreign currency, which he'd discovered when he'd helped her carry in a new mattress for her guest bedroom. She'd papered an entire wall with German francs, Japanese yens, Costa Rican colones, and others he didn't recognize. Most of them were colored copies, she'd said with a shrug. Debi also liked bottle caps, which wasn't strange in itself—he'd heard of people with bottle cap collections—except she'd epoxied hundreds of them to her mudroom floor. Mick wondered what other surprises he'd discover about her as they got to know each other.

They paddled the boat as close to shore as they could, then Mick pulled it to higher ground. Water lapped against the sides, singing a liquid lullaby. Debi hopped out of the boat, the quilted throw under one arm, and spread it onto the least rocky spot she could find. They worked quietly alongside one another, Mick tending the canoe, and Debi unpacking their thermos of coffee and freshly baked scones.

When he finally sat down, Debi took his hand and gave it a little squeeze.

"This was a nice surprise. Thank you."

"You're welcome." Mick sat down next to her, reveling in the effect her smile had on him. After watching Debi from a distance for so long, he still couldn't believe they were together. It could have happened sooner, she teased him a week earlier. If he had come in a few times on his own, without Stella, and when the shop wasn't so busy, Debi might have come to the realization much sooner.

"I think it was good timing on our part. You know, getting together now rather than earlier," Debi said quietly. She must have read his mind. "I mean, it would have been nice to get to know you sooner, but the timing is kind of uncanny."

Mick squinted at a distant point near town. Vehicles moved like insects along Highway 61 on the hill above Hendricks. He looked down at her hand in his. It was so right, so perfect, it nearly choked him with emotion.

"How so?"

"I think Gretchen might have gotten me to sell if you weren't around to talk some sense into me," she said, pulling her collar tight around her neck. "Have you heard what her next step is?"

"I've heard whisperings that she's going to unload Lost Pine Mine and focus on her other prospects out of town. Consolidated Iron doesn't want it, so it's not likely she'll get what she'd hoped for from anyone else." He uncapped the thermos and poured the steaming coffee into two cups. "I think the property as is up there is too insignificant to mine by itself. Your property would have made developing it worthwhile."

Mick leaned back on his hands, stretching his legs before him. "You wouldn't have sold it. Once you thought about it, you would have realized it."

"That check was pretty tempting though."

"I can imagine."

He never asked her the amount of Gretchen's offer, and Debi didn't volunteer it. Maybe she was embarrassed she'd turned it down, or maybe she figured it didn't matter. Either way Mick never doubted she'd refuse it. Her sense of family and loyalty was what he loved about her most.

Debi cleared her throat. "Speaking of 'tempting'—"

Mick leaned toward her. He breathed in the sugary scent, a quality of hers he'd grown to love the more time he spent with her. It was a heady distraction, one he took comfort in more and more each day. He was in love with "The Donut Lady" as Stella liked to call her now when Stella and he were by themselves. Six months ago, he wouldn't have believed it possible. To Mick, his from-a-distance infatuation with Debi Thomas was a dream come true.

Her lips curved and parted slightly. Mick leaned closer.

As he grazed her lips, Mick knew that no matter how many years passed, he'd always hunger for her kiss. The kiss was searing yet sweet, its softness sparking a fierce passion that coursed through him. Debi's lips held an underlying urgency that almost stopped his breath. His hand found the back of her neck and he pulled her gently to him, their kiss deepening.

A gull's cry a few minutes later pulled them apart when he startled. Silently, Mick cursed the bird.

Debi licked her bottom lip. "Maybe I can miss my book club," she said in a husky voice.

"After Donna Marconi got everyone to agree to a new time just for you? A dangerous thought."

"You're right. I can't do that." She let her fingers trace a line along his jaw. "But after book club, my day is free."

"And Stella is spending the night with a friend, so—"

Debi's smile was wicked. "So there's plenty of time later—"

He snapped his fingers. "I almost forgot. Stella wants you to read something of hers."

She sat upright, her face brightening. "Seriously? That gets me right here." Debi tapped her chest.

"Except I must have left it at home." Mick dipped his hand inside his jacket, patted his pants pockets, searching for the paper Stella handed him that morning. "You'll have to wait until later. Sorry."

Debi slumped, but the smile lingered. "If you told me a few months ago Stella would be sharing her writing with me, I wouldn't have believed it." Debi gave him a sidelong glance. "She gets it from you, you know. The writing talent."

"I guess I'll take credit for that." He chucked a pebble into the water. Ripples fanned along the surface.

"When did you start writing poetry?"

"In high school. But I never used my own name on them."

"Really? What a waste of talent."

Mick checked to see if she were joking. "I'm pretty high on the amateur scale."

"So I guess I shouldn't brag that the infamous Silas Penn, aka Mick Graham, has been leaving me love poems at the bakery this whole time?"

Mick chuckled and shook his head fiercely. "Silas Penn likes his anonymity."

Debi scooted closer to him on the blanket so they sat hip to hip. A breeze washed over them, the air scented with fish, algae, and a hint of smoke from Red's outdoor grill that he fired up daily for the restaurant's lunch hour barbeque. She pulled her knees up and hugged them to her chest with one arm. Mick watched her rummage through the rocks beside her with her other hand, stacking a few flat-bottomed ones into a cairn while she hummed.

"How is Stella handling the problems with Gretchen?"

Mick thought for a moment. "Stella is pretty stubborn. She also has a strong sense of loyalty. When Gretchen tried pumping her for information about what you'd do with your property, Stella knew she was being used. Naturally, that ticked her off."

"Has she talked with her grandmother since the argument?"

"Yes, a little. I think they'll both come around. Gretchen

needed a wake-up call. Stella is her granddaughter, not her business partner." He picked through the rocks beside him, tossing them one by one into the water. "She wants to be a twelve-year-old and do teen things. That doesn't include going to board meetings."

"Poor Stella. Adults can be such jerks sometimes."

"If any good has come from this, it's that Stella is confiding in me more."

"That's huge, especially at her age."

Mick shrugged off his jacket, balling it behind him to support his head as he stretched out on the blanket. Debi planted a hand beside his head and leaning over him, looked into his eyes.

"I would have loved to watch you raise her."

"I would have loved that too." Mick twisted a lock of her hair around his finger when it brushed against his face, tickling his cheek. "It's not too late, you know. To watch me." He watched her smile broaden as she read into his meaning. Debi's eyes matched the sky above her head— clear and hopeful.

"I would love to."

One Year Later

༺❀༻

Debi bumbled through the front door of the shop, her arms wrapped around a tub of serving ware from a weekend event at Blueberry Point Lodge. A line of customers stretched from the front counter to the door. Luckily, Matt Stetman stood at the end of the line and noticed her coming. He held open the door.

"Morning, sunshine," he said. His expression was overly animated, even for Matt.

"Good morning." Debi glanced around, wondering if she'd missing something. The shop was packed, like standing-room-only packed. "What's going on?"

Matt made a show of looking around, then shrugged. "Beats me. The town wants donuts, I guess."

"Hi, Debi."

Debi heard Stella's voice before she saw her. Behind Debi, at the table in the bay window, Stella sat slumped in the chair, her feet up on another. Her usual jelly donut and a carton of chocolate milk sat in front of her.

"Well...hi!" Debi looked around, but she couldn't see over the heads of those in line to the other side of the shop. Mick was nowhere in sight. "Did you come with your dad?"

Her smile was overdone, almost cartoonish. "He dropped me off. Had something to do."

Now she was stumped. They always came together. Mick hadn't mentioned anything out of the ordinary on today's schedule. "Is he coming back to take you to school?"

"Probably." Stella was too chipper. Something was definitely up.

"Okay, well, let me know if you need a ride over to school. In the meantime, I better get to work."

The line parted for Debi even before she could excuse herself. The oversized box in her arms must have done the trick. Behind the counter, Holly and Ronnie looked frazzled but in control.

"What's going on?" Debi whispered when Holly bent over at the case to fill an order.

"I'm not really sure," Holly mumbled. "I hope we don't run out."

"That's never happened before, even during special events in the summer." Debi scanned the shop. May wasn't even officially the busy season—a few more weeks before Memorial Day—so these weren't even tourists. "Let me put this stuff in the back, then I'll fill orders."

Debi walked into the back room and noticed the three rolling racks right away. Each of them was six feet tall and

ALL were filled, top to bottom shelf, with glazed rings. She would never make that many unless she had a special order, which had never happened for this amount. A quick glance at the bulletin board where she kept order tickets confirmed it: No one had ordered glazed rings. There had to be at least three hundred of the things. What a huge waste this would be! Surely, it was a mistake. And why had Holly and Ronnie come here in the middle of the night without telling her? Something was *definitely* up.

Ronnie rushed back, slid an empty tray into the sink and just as quickly took a tray from one of the rolling racks.

Debi stopped him. "Ronnie, when did all these rings get made and why?"

Ronnie's eyes popped open as wide as donut holes and called over his shoulder. "Better ask Holly."

She set the box on the floor and marched to the front counter. Holly handed out rings over the counter straight from the trays, two at a time. Ronnie did the same at the other end of the counter. The front door was now wide open, the line spilling out onto the sidewalk.

What is going on?

"Hey."

It was Mick. Somehow he'd snaked his way through the crowd and leaned against the counter. Mick crossed his arms, looking pretty relaxed, considering she was about to implode.

"This is crazy. What's going on in town?" she asked, but her attention turned to the cash register. It was alarmingly quiet with all the activity. "And why is everyone getting FREE donuts? Hold on."

Holly was a robot, stooping to retrieve donuts from the case as fast as she passed them over the counter. And the line continued to grow. Debi touched Holly's arm to stop the madness. The shop was bleeding donuts.

"Please stop and tell me what's happening, Holly. Why all the donuts? And why are we giving them away?"

Holly did stop. She could hardly keep the grin off her face. "You should probably ask him." She jabbed at the air with a ring in her hand, toward Mick, who still looked maddening cool standing across the way. "Oh, and someone left a poem on the counter awhile ago."

"A poem?"

Holly's grinned broadened.

"Where is it?"

She pointed to the bulletin board near the door.

Debi came from behind the counter, shooting Mick a look, knowing he was responsible for turning Debi's Donuts into Grand Central Crazy somehow. His grin only widened.

"I thought Silas Penn was finished leaving poems around here?" she said under her breath.

"Maybe he wants a little attention after all."

As if on cue, Matt Stetman let out an ear-splitting whistle. Honestly, everyone had lost their minds. Debi sank back against the counter next to Mick, shocked into watching this circus unfold.

Matt plucked a yellow paper from the bulletin board and handed it with great flourish to Stella. She stood on the chair, flipped her hair over both shoulders, and cleared her throat.

Debi clutched Mick's arm. "If that's your poem, I think

she's going to read it. She's not going to tell everyone it's you, is she, Mick?"

"She wouldn't dare."

Matt waved his arms, and the place went as quiet as a library.

"What is—?"

"Please. Just listen." Mick gave her a look so meaningful it made her catch her breath.

Debi was still looking at him when Stella started talking.

"Everyone knows my dad isn't a very talkative guy, right? He's kinda quiet, actually," she said, and murmurs of affirmation floated up. "But that doesn't mean he doesn't have important things to say. And believe me, this IS important."

Then Stella zeroed in on Debi, and Debi knew. She pressed her hand against her chest.

"So he wrote a poem for someone."

"Tell the truth," Mick scolded lightheartedly.

Debi could see the color rise on Stella's neck from across the room.

"Okay, I helped write it." Another look at Debi, a lopsided grin.

Debi could hardly breathe.

Stella giggled, then licked her lips, and lifted her chin:

"There once was a ranger named Mick,
Who needed a wife to pick
So he gathered the town
Bought donuts all around
But getting her to say 'yes' was the trick."

Stella crossed her arms, waiting.

The shop was so quiet.

"Mick," she whispered. Debi could feel Mick watching her, but she couldn't look away from Stella's eager expression.

"Well?" Mick's voice was soft.

Debi didn't know whether to laugh or give in to the lump in her throat. There were so many eyes on them, people waiting for what happened next, and Donna Marconi right in front, clasping her hands and mouthing the words "say yes."

Debi turned to him. "So what trick will get you the answer you want?"

He shrugged. "There's no trick. It rhymed with 'Mick' and 'pick.'"

"But—"

He put a finger to her lips, which made Debi smile. She'd always talked too much when she was nervous. She was weightless, buoyed by air. "Yes. A hundred times yes."

Mick held up a tiny white velvet box and opened it to show her the ring. "I almost forgot this at home."

Debi laughed aloud. "It would have been fine. We're surrounded by so many rings today."

"True." His grin was wide. "You're sure?"

Debi heard Stella whoop in the background. Behind the counter, Holly and Ronnie resumed passing out donuts.

"I'm sure," she said. "Trust me."

· · ·

ARE YOU READY TO READ LOVE LIKE FOREVER, Book #4?

Acknowledgments

Thank you to Bianca Blythe, K. Kris Loomis, Jenny Finlayson, and Katelyn Leishman for reading early versions of this story. I appreciate your time and insight into making this a better book.

Thank you to Hollie Westring for your editing prowess. You are appreciated more than I can put into words, which is not an easy admission for a writer.

Thank you to Jenny Zemanek at Seedlings Design Studio for another stunning cover.

As always, my family has been instrumental in my ability to write stories. Without your love, support, and understanding for spending unnatural periods of time in front of a screen, bookmaking would not be possible.

Also by D.E. Malone

Hearts in Hendricks series

Love Like Water

Love Like Fire

Love Like Air

Love Like Forever

Blueberry Point Romance series

Love, Lies and Lavender

Love, Lies and Mistletoe

Love, Lies and Lullabies

Love, Lies and Lemon Pie

Blueberry Point Romance Collection (novellas)

Love Between the Lines (free novella)

A Forever Kiss in Silver Leaf Falls, Book #5

For the latest book happenings, special subscriber giveaways, and advance notice on sales and new releases, subscribe to D.E. Malone's newsletter, Welcome to the Sweet Life or visit her website at www.demalone.com to sign up.

About the Author

D.E. Malone writes sweet contemporary romance and is the author of the Hearts in Hendricks and Blueberry Point romance series. She also writes for middle grade audiences under Dawn Malone, and is the author of BINGO SUMMER and THE UPSIDE OF DOWN. Her work has appeared in Highlights for Children, Pockets, and the Chicken Soup for the Soul series. She loves traveling to places off the beaten path which inspire the small-town settings in her stories. When she's not writing, she enjoys reading, hiking, and continuing her never-ending quest for the holy grail of bakeries. Visit D.E. at her website to sign up for her newsletter. There you'll find a full list of her books.

If you'd like to join a book-loving community of readers, why not join D.E. Malone's private group on Facebook? Help her name new characters, get the advance scoop on book news and giveaways, and meet other bookish friends. We hope you'll join us!

She's also on Instagram, Pinterest and Goodreads @dmalonebooks.

f **⊙**